SMALL
STATIONS
FICTION

Anxos SUMAI

# HARVEST MOON

Published in 2020 by
SMALL STATIONS PRESS
20 Dimitar Manov Street, 1408 Sofia, Bulgaria
You can order books and contact the publisher at
www.smallstations.com



This book was first published in the Galician language as *A lúa da colleita* by Editorial Galaxia (Vigo, 2013). A list of our fiction titles can be found at www.smallstations.com/fiction

*This work received a grant from the Directorate-General for Cultural Policies of the Ministry of Culture and Tourism of the Xunta de Galicia in the call for translation and/or publishing grants of the year 2019*

*Esta obra recibiu unha axuda da Dirección Xeral de Políticas Culturais da Consellería de Cultura e Turismo da Xunta de Galicia na convocatoria de axudas para a tradución e/ou edición do ano 2019*

ISBN 978-954-384-104-2

Anxos SUMAI

# *Harvest Moon*

WINNER OF THE GARCÍA BARROS AWARD AND OF THE SPANISH CRITICS' PRIZE FOR GALICIAN FICTION

Translated from Galician by Carys EVANS-CORRALES

Small Stations Press

*To O.-D., in the dark light.*

*I hear the night train every evening*
*Maybe change is coming soon*
*With the harvest moon.*

Bedlam, 'Harvest Moon'

*I can lose nothing that is myself*
*I can do nothing against this instant.*

Olalla Cociña, *No Precipice*

# 1

The little creature turned around and around within an eggshell, or perhaps coming to life in the heart of a grain of wheat, or perhaps in a mother's womb. It floated endlessly, weightlessly about. Sometimes it would be dragged from that timeless zone and would adopt the form of a little girl nibbling at an apple at midnight, or taking on the yellow light of dead peaches. She might one day become a tissue-paper kite, flying in loops over blackthorns and evergreens. Or a frog inside a stone.

It's not unusual for the little creature to manifest itself in the form in which people want to see her. Not even if the person seeing her closes her eyes, the little creature disappears and returns to that place where she lives – timeless and with no defined forms.

## 2

Some afternoons at the end of the term when it was hot, Nuria and Quin would cut their classes at High School and go off to the beach. They would take an hour's walk from the town to a small, semicircular inlet with smooth, gray sand. During the final weeks of spring, there were still no bathers there: those preferred the large beach about three hundred yards distant from the bay. The large beach was a broad band, also of gray sand, but more open, and not suddenly cut off by a high, rough jetty. This jetty, which impeded access into the sea by stretching out into it, allowed Nuria and Quin to enjoy a certain amount of intimacy, though they often had to share it with the seagulls.

They sunbathed in the nude, swam, making love somewhat hurriedly and inexpertly, and, moved more by the need to satisfy their desire than by the enjoyment of learning to caress each other, they would lie in the sand absolutely worn out, looking surprised and incredulous when that first sexual experience was coming to an end. In the air, the sharp scent of semen and sweat was mixed with the echoes of a colony of small children and with the chocolate and oranges they each carried in their bags. Hers was a military backpack that her elder brother had given her. There was semen on their bellies; in her mouth, the taste of chalk from his penis. They were still kids, and Quin was left stretched out on a damp towel, wearing a certain idiotic expression. She, naked and glowing, let herself be swept by the force of the waves, her entire body open under the cloudless sky. Without actually caressing each other, their loins were pressed against each other under the force of a greedy satisfaction.

Later, as the sun began to set, they took their sandwiches from Nuria's knapsack, passing mouthfuls to each other with their tongues. Those were beautiful evenings, when no one missed them. Nobody saw them either, and if anyone – a fisherman steering his boat towards the beach, or a photographer who'd appear every now and then to take photos of the estuary – looked at them reproachfully, Nuria and Quin would issue forth guffaws, as if drunk with insolence. But one afternoon, from the stony path that surrounded the large beach, they noticed people working at the top of the jetty. They were lifting a small wooden building and unloading construction material. Days later, they would see a huge poster on the street, showing a photograph of the plan of the building and an advertisement for apartments for sale. It made them sad to see the end of those happy days, the evenings when the virgin sand retained only their footsteps and the traces of their bodies entwined in love, just as they erased only the star-shaped traces of seagulls' feet.

All the same, Nuria felt somewhat envious of that building, which had still not become anything. She looked at it covetously. She imagined herself living in one of its highest apartments, whose view would probably include the ocean. And if she didn't manage to distinguish the ocean, she would certainly see the little islands which, like a rosary made from their stone masses with hardly any vegetation, protected the estuary from the Atlantic storms.

'Someday I'll live in one of those apartments,' she said to Quin with conviction. Quin was walking ahead of her, kicking at the water. She, behind him, was gathering up her straight black hair into a small bun above her neck.

Every day since the workers had begun to dig the foundation, there were more people going for walks around the area than ever and they no longer bathed in the nude. They didn't even kiss or pass mouthfuls to each other.

'So why would you want to live there? It's awful. And what's more, it's only meant for foreigners.'

'I'd like to know what the view is from the top, to gaze out of the window and keep at it all day long, just looking out. That would be *my* house.'

'So wouldn't it be the same house for both of us: *our* house?'

The boy's words surprised Nuria. It had never occurred to her to share any other places with him that weren't their high school classroom, the cinema where they spent Sunday afternoons, and the beach. She found it impossible to intuit that there might be another spot that belonged to just the two of them. Such an idea never even entered her head. And that made her sense the unnerving vertigo of a totally empty future.

They had just been in for a dip, and had lain down on the sand, with its coastline exposed to the evening sun. A group of bottle-nosed dolphins broke the surface of the sea near the beach. Quin stroked Nuria distractedly and smoked a cigarette, waiting for an answer to the question that had been hanging in the air since before they'd been in the sea.

'And so the house won't be for the two of us?' he insisted.

But Nuria didn't give a verbal answer... she turned around on the towel and lay on her back, avoiding all contact with him.

'It's time we were off,' she said, standing up.

Somehow, that unexpected question altered the pure happiness of those months, and Nuria was shaken with foreboding. She didn't know what it was, but there was something strange in the wind, something that even seemed to change the color of the evening, and the voices of the men working high up on the precipice became sharper and made her feel uncomfortable. That something she was sensing, something she could neither name nor give a particular form to, began to turn Quin's face into that of the child he was: beardless, and with pimples on his nose. The drops of sweat accumulated on his growing mustache and body, which was too thin and as slippery as an eel, slithered onto the towel as he stood up. Without shape, without muscles. Nuria suddenly rejected both his kisses and his presence. It was as if she had abandoned her childhood in a fraction of a second, and the ingenuous smile on her face disappeared forever, together with the essence of what was still left in a little girl's gaze.

'Why should it be *our* house?'

They argued. He was under the impression that Nuria wasn't Nuria anymore. She'd become suddenly aggressive, challenging him with reddened eyes fighting to leave their orbits and insisting on pushing him, pummeling her fists into his chest. Furiously, without being capable of understanding that burst of ire, Quin picked up his things and walked over to the street. Nuria did not follow him. She brushed off the sand that had stuck to her body and dressed calmly. She gathered up her hair, tying it in a knot with the printed bandana under which her long mane continued to be held in place until the term was over... a Portuguese kerchief that had been a gift from her mother. Instead of walking towards the street and following Quin, she decided to return by the path of earth and stones around the edge of the beach. It would take more time, but she wanted to be alone. She felt strange, as if a kind of mist were invading her little by little while the countryside lost its consistency. She looked at the building under construction, and it seemed to her to be floating in the air, and that the precipice had turned into a flat, faded drawing. She looked for Quin and saw him walking along the street. Then she thought she heard his voice, but wasn't sure whether he was calling out to her or whether he was still breathing into her ear, like when they were lying on the sand. She felt irritated, uncomfortable, as if her clothes were too tight. Her salt-covered skin smelled different... it smelled of a sudden, short-lived outburst of rain and wind. Disturbed, she started walking, her knapsack on her back and the towel tied around her hips.

* * *

She woke up with a shocking headache. With her eyes closed, she brought her hand to her forehead and felt her hair. It was soaking wet. Actually, she was wet all over, clothes included. Terrified, she noticed cuts on her face, on her arms, on her legs. She felt sharp pains from open wounds and the throbbing of bruises. Frightened, she tried to open her eyes, but her eyelids weighed too heavily and insisted on closing. She realized she was lying down somewhere that swayed gently in the air. She thought she was dreaming, and tried to accommodate herself to the movement that rocked her to sleep and woke her up once she had controlled it. But the pain was so intolerable and she felt so cold she couldn't possibly be dreaming. She sat up and opened her eyes in excruciating pain. A pale circle of light reflected over the surface of a dark liquid that covered her legs.

*Water. Am I in the water?*

Alarmed, she tried to straighten herself up, and the luminous circle moved over to her, to the spot she'd leaned on to stand up. Stupefied, she then realized she was on a boat, and that the circle of light was the moon. Looking around, the tranquil moonlight was shining on the water. She saw lights rising and falling to the rhythm of the waves at some distance in front of her. She calculated she must be in the middle of the sea. She was about to scream, but she didn't scream, paralyzed by sudden panic. Something behind her, in the part of the boat she couldn't see, was watching her. She knew it was watching her. She turned slowly around, as if afraid to wake up, and directly caught sight of the profile of a seagull perched on the edge of the boat. The bird was so still, she herself remained immobile, just looking at it. It was an immaculate white, with its yellow beak turned to the sunrise. It looked so incredibly beautiful she was frightened again, but even more so when she saw the blood sliding down the bird's feet. Then she became conscious of the wounds on her arms, her broken fingernails, her pecked shoulders. But she had no clue as to what she was doing there, and hadn't the slightest idea why she was submerged under water with open wounds on her body. Her nails were hideously torn, as if she'd been in a really bad fight; her body was beaten to a pulp, as if she had been thrust by the waves of a ferocious sea against the tall, rugged rocks. She had sand in her mouth, and the skin of her knees was scraped from having been dragged, goodness knows where.

The lights moved on the edge of the sea. She looked around and saw she was near a small island. She stood up and leapt into the sea, and the sea didn't cover her. The land was just a few steps away. With the sea at thigh level, she walked up to a nearby rock. Then she looked out for the seagull, to feel again the peace of the white seagull perched on the boat. And there it was, motionless in the same spot, displaying its profile. It was just that the new profile was no longer as white or as immaculate: it looked ragged, as if its wing had been torn off, as if its flesh had been pulled off by teeth. The fleshless bones looked almost as clean as the shining feathers of its right profile, if not for the blood that covered it from head to foot. She noticed a sweet taste in her mouth and licked away a sticky substance on the edges of her lips. Obstinately, she wiped her mouth with both hands and, when she looked at them again, she saw the blood had set almost into a callus.

That was when she screamed.

And once she'd finished screaming, it wasn't long before she thought she heard someone splashing about in the sea. Oars. Someone was rowing in her direction. Voices. The voices of men. *Who's that over there?* In a few minutes, two boats had caught up with her, with two sailors in each boat. Incredulously, the sailors saw the injured seagull and the girl in torn clothing, sitting among the rocks. The girl was trembling with cold, or perhaps fear. One of the sailors threw a winter coat over her while the other three gazed at her as if they'd seen a ghost. In a pliable and unresisting silence, Nuria allowed herself to be rowed to one of the secondary boats, suddenly concerned about what those men might be thinking, because they'd asked her what had happened and she didn't know what to say; they'd inquired what her name was, and she didn't know. Until a bright pilot light burst into action in her head and she murmured something unintelligible.

'What are you saying, little one?' asked the sailor who'd covered her up.

'It was here, it was here...'

'The seagull? Seagulls never do any harm.'

'No, not the seagull. It...'

But she couldn't go on speaking, as she was beginning to vomit and felt as if she were throwing up something black and abrasive. The abrasive thing was what seemed to be covering her skin, as if she lived inside an animal. The black thing was the conviction that she was beginning to be possessed when she lost sight of the wounded seagull; both she and the seagull had disappeared together, suddenly, like a hologram.

There was something within her at that moment that wouldn't allow her to find herself either in time or in space, much less in memory. As if she, Nuria, were one of those little black, abrasive islands that rose in the middle of the estuary at low tide and disappeared without a trace when the tide was high.

And yet they were always there.

# 3

In mid-July there occurred one of those things that made her furious: in the closet at the entrance she found an orange wig which, evidently, wasn't hers. When she didn't find a logical explanation for things that startled her in her own house, she became angst-ridden and couldn't fall asleep. In cases like that, when the angst came on during the night, she'd call Rubén, her brother.

'It's a tad shopworn,' she explained to him. 'Can you see me in a wig like that... a clown's wig? Not even at a carnival, man. Impossible! It was on the coat-hanger, looking as innocent as anything. I spent all day trying to figure out who could have brought it in, but no luck! I fell asleep, woke up, and here I am now, holding it in my hand. It's not that I donned it for some party or other! What do you think?'

'I don't know, love,' answered her brother, worn out, deprived of any concern, accustomed to being woken up by Nuria in the wee hours of the morning. 'And might it be...?'

'Who?' shouted Nuria into the phone. 'How could you think of her now, man? Don't get all worked up, it's been ages since she set foot in this house.'

'Shh, love,' said Rubén, lowering his voice. 'Shh, go to sleep and an explanation will come to you. Come on! Listen, lower your voice even more until it's a murmur: *Until tomorrow, good night, sleep well, goodbye.*'

When Rubén spoke to her in that sweet, almost childlike tone, repeating that tender litany he'd recited to her ever since she was little, Nuria felt as if someone was working on a particular point on her neck, and began to calm down, just like a cat when its head is being fondled. She left the wig on the floor and sank among the sheets with the telephone jammed to her ear. She made herself comfortable in a fetal position and closed her eyes. With her brother's voice at the other end of the line, she was asleep in no time at all.

From time to time, while still asleep, she would roll over in the bed and thump against the wall, as if defending herself against a violent enemy. Then she'd fall silent, sleeping peacefully and perfectly still, but, a little before dawn, one of her greatest terrors would fall upon her. She tried to open her eyes and couldn't. She tried to move her arms about and couldn't. She tried to move her legs, turn around in her bed, and couldn't. She tried to open her mouth to pronounce some word that would wake her up, and couldn't do that either. But she would breathe and listen to her heart beating. She thought, as she always did whenever her sleep came to a halt, that she was suffering from one of those cataleptic episodes in horror stories and was being buried alive. She tried to control her panic. If she managed to open her eyes a tiny bit to see the light, she would be safe and sound.

Then the telephone under the pillow began to ring, and its persistent sound woke up her entire body. At last her eyelids obeyed the brain's commands and she was able to open her eyes.

'Rubén, is that you?'

But it wasn't. A doubtful voice asked if she was Nuria Uría.

'Yes.'

'This is Xoaquín.' The caller fell silent, as if waiting for Nuria to answer.

'Xoaquín?' she asked sleepily.

'Yes, Xoaquín Cuns, from the real estate agency.' The voice became cold, almost aggressive. 'I'm calling about your renting the apartment.'

Nuria looked at the watch on the little bedside table. It was half-past eight in the morning. She rubbed her eyes, freed herself of the sheets, and sat on the bed. She put one foot on the wig that she'd left on the floor the previous night. It was soft, and felt like the hair of a child. She got up and went off to the kitchen with the phone in her hand. She heard Xoaquín Cuns typing away at a computer as he forced her to come to a decision about renting an apartment at the beach. Nuria didn't have the slightest idea what he was talking about. And yet there was something familiar in that voice, and it wasn't long before she had formed a particular image in her mind, a very precise one, of the apartment and the countryside around it. She picked up a glass, placed a vitamin C pill at the bottom, and filled it under the tap in the sink. As she observed the water turning yellow and its bubbles ascending to the surface, she decided she needed a vacation. She had begun to postpone them, tired out from traveling almost every week from Madrid to Lisbon, of waking up some days in that little apartment that had belonged to her parents, and others in the room of a pink boarding house in the Portuguese city. She didn't have to think twice: that unexpected call inspired her to make a decision.

'Yes, of course. I'll be there on July 31st.'

'It'll be on the fifth floor. The apartment on the fourth is still occupied.'

Nuria, still confused by her sudden awakening and enraptured by the fizzy bubbles, kept silent.

'Is there some problem?'

'No, that's fine.'

Xoaquín Cuns hung up. Nuria tried to adjust to the hurried decision she had just made as she drank the glass of vitaminized water.

* * *

In a corner of the patio, the lemon tree remained immobile despite the sudden thundering of the summer storm. It hadn't rained yet, but against the west, towards the estuary, the sky was turning green and a fierce windstorm from a dense gray cloud threatened to engulf the cusp of the hill, the village inhabiting its slope, and the exotic hotel of little pink and cinnamon houses that was cropping up in a clearing on Mount Xiabre.

'Hey, Happy, wouldn't it be better if we went inside?' an old man in a shirt and a pair of wrinkled linen trousers asked of a blonde girl sitting on the grass.

She didn't need to answer, because it wasn't long before raindrops as large as tears began to fall, and the people walking around the patio or just beginning to nod off on the grass sought cover under the house supports that served as a reception area and a restaurant. A flash of lightning electrified the lemon tree, and a dog dragged itself off until it reached the girl.

'*Come on, Iggy, come in,*' Happy patted the dog, who then hid himself under the chair the girl had been sitting on. '*Ça va, ça va?*'

They sat down and watched the rain, listening to the thunder retreating over the estuary.

'Let's hope it's just a passing thunderstorm.'

'Well, I like thunderstorms,' observed a man in English. 'When I've been walking for several days and I get hit by a rainstorm like this one... Ooh! It makes me feel great!'

'Luis, please bring us something to drink. Okay, darling?'

A tall, burly young man went into the house and came out again with beers for everyone.

'Would you like one, Ivo?' he offered it to the man who'd confessed to being thrilled in thunderstorms.

Ivo drank down his beer in long swigs, Happy caressed hers for a while between her hands, until the fine layer of ice covering the bottle had disappeared. Vidal, the man dressed in linen, left his on the table.

'There are vagabonds and vagabonds,' Ivo began again. 'I'm one of the vagabonds that walk the Earth from end to end. That's what my life consists of: walking.'

No one paid him any attention: Vidal because he didn't understand much English, and Luis and Happy because they were used to Ivo cogitating out loud.

'Do you guys know why I walk?' he then remained quiet for a moment, concentrating on the rain that was falling ever more furiously. 'I walk to find perfect solitude.'

The lemon tree shook itself with a sudden gust of wind. Ivo shut his eyes, got out of his chair, and ran to the middle of the patio. Under the rain, he began to dance like a solitary Indian in a huge meadow. Vidal disappeared and returned a short while later with a camera, and, possessed by an overbearing need to amass images of that moment, took ceaseless photos of Ivo.

'I think it's going to rain a lot this summer,' said Luis, bending over to kiss Happy's mouth.

* * *

That place was the end of the world to her, or that was what she'd have liked to think during the previous two years. It would have been the definitive place to establish herself because, apart from that place, she knew full well there was nothing other than urban legends and imaginary beings – stories of people who go around and around in a scenography that can only be called pathetic. Beyond her end of the world she knew there were enormous meadows, covered with ripened wheat and poppies, mountains from which no one can fall, planets of pure diamond, and industrial machinery that changed peaches into jam.

But that was not to be. It was no longer enough for her to have a table full of what was once necessary to satisfy the brain's hunger. It seemed she wanted more and was no longer gratified. Not even that man with light eyes and a brown mane, the one who stood up to look at her, pushing away with his hand an enormous black plastic curtain that divided off the space he had chosen for painting... not even he was good enough for her. She knew him too well: he no longer surprised nor stimulated her. She had worn him out, as one wears out a gold mine and ought to procure another one to exploit. With no lamenting, no excessive clinging, and no nostalgia or *alharacas*.

'*Alharaca*.' She thought about the word that seemed so pleasantly employed for the man who had observed her, trying to discover its meaning.

She wanted to collect her things and leave as soon as possible. But then again, it would be better not to take anything with her until she knew where she would settle down. For a while she could do without the books, the CDs, the computer, the sculpture of the babies by her friend Carlos. She could also do without the huge mural she was working on. The same went for the trunk bursting with whips, ropes, mirrors stained with the remnants of cocaine, a silver sniffer, the box where she kept the heroin and all that world of irreverence, violence, and exploration of the limits of pain and pleasure that was her most beloved treasure, and which so bothered the man who kept watching her, even with the black plastic curtain clutched in his hand.

The previous day she'd told him she was leaving, and he took it the only way possible: without reproaches or violence, as if they were two travelers who, after a time of sharing the challenges, the beauty, and the secrets of the road, had to return to their homes.

'Where are you going?' he'd asked her, aware she was already excluding him from any decision.

'I don't know... well, I'm not too sure. To tell you the truth, I'm not very sure of anything.'

'Will you tell me as soon as you know?'

'Of course. I'll call you as soon as I've moved in.'

'I'll always love you so much, Bet.'

'And I you. Also. I love you also, Tomás.'

But maybe she'd never call him. What for? She should leave that end of the world behind. She should find another.

# 4

Nuria Uría reached the station at five in the afternoon. She got off the train empty-handed, wearing a long skirt gathered at the waist over a baggy white shirt. She didn't carry a handbag or baggage of any kind. In her hands she held several five-thousand peseta bills, clenched between her fingers. A metal pendant in the shape of a large stylized heart dangled from a thin silver chain, beating against her breasts as she walked, and every so often she would hold it as if trying to protect it.

She seemed to know perfectly well where she was going, because on leaving the station she simply followed the street that led to the center of town. She stopped at a shoe store, where she exchanged the platform sandals she was wearing for some blue canvas slippers.

'Would you mind if I left the sandals here?'

'Don't worry, I'll give you a bag to carry them in.'

'I don't want to carry them.' She said this with such emphasis and certainty that the sales associate looked at her in bewilderment: the sandals were new and were really pretty.

Nuria left the sandals as a pair, on the sofa that had been moved to where she'd been sitting. She left. The sales assistant approached them with some misgivings before prudently picking them up with her fingertips. They were covered in green moiré, giving off blue and yellow flashes with the light that came in through the window display. She couldn't understand how someone could leave behind such lovely, expensive footwear. She took a good look at them and no, there was nothing odd about them. She checked their size on the soles. A seven and a half. She was delighted, because it just happened to be the size she wore. There were no rules forbidding her to wear shoes that customers didn't want, but just in case, she agreed it would be wiser to wait a few weeks in case that woman changed her mind.

Nuria's hurried steps led her to the square in which the real estate agency was located, where she'd agreed to rent the apartment. She stopped at a clothing store before picking up the keys to the new apartment. She bought a pair of blue jeans and an anodyne, short-sleeved, olive-green t-shirt. She left her skirt, blouse, and underwear properly folded inside the plastic bag she'd been given when she paid for them.

As soon as she left, she went into the agency. She was in a hurry, but didn't want to appear nervous. She concealed her anxiety by doing mental mathematics to bring her body to a sudden halt. Motionless, in the middle of the office, she asked for Xoaquín Cuns. There were two desks, one of them occupied by an older man, whom Nuria approached. At the other, a younger, bearded, and smaller man was attending to a couple selling an apartment. The older man pointed at the younger one and asked Nuria if she didn't mind waiting. She replied she was in a hurry and was only there to collect some keys. She looked truly harried, in spite of the delay and having to stand stock-still. The man extended his hand and directed her to a chair upholstered in faded brown corduroy.

'Please sit down. I'm Fernando.'

Nuria shook his hand.

'I'm Nuria Uría.'

Upon hearing the woman's name, the young man looked at her from a distance, almost with dislike. He nonetheless greeted her and apologized for not being able to attend to her at that moment, but he gestured to his co-worker, where the contract was kept and above all, the keys. Nuria paid a month in advance. She rejected his offer to escort her to the apartment, as if she knew perfectly well where it was located. Without looking at her, Xoaquín Cuns gave her an enigmatic farewell:

'Welcome once more.'

'Goodbye,' she answered, without acknowledging the contempt in his voice.

Nuria left without paying further mind to what that Xoaquín Cuns had just said, surely a rhetorical formula he used with his customers. He looked over-worked, too concerned with the sale of the apartment he was working on. Even so, something about his voice sounded familiar to her again, like when he'd called her. But it wasn't that. Nuria felt that almost everything seemed familiar and also, what with her nerves, her hurry, her anxiety, she misunderstood what people said to her. That made her immediately forget the man's commentary, and she left the agency tense and nervous, just as she'd entered it. When they were alone, Fernando addressed his colleague sarcastically, as if they'd spoken about that woman on other occasions.

'What? Is that her, then?'

Xoaquín Cuns blushed and scratched his beard under his jaw, shrugging his shoulders with indifference.

The two of them looked through the window that gave onto the street. They saw Nuria Uría deciding which direction to take. Shortly after that they lost sight of her, and got back to their work.

She walked decidedly along a commercial street crammed with people. There was a moment when, as she turned a corner, her pendant struck her heart, and she chose to reduce the rhythm of her strides. She stopped, and, surprised, asked herself how it was she knew what road to take if she hadn't been back to the town for twenty years, and it was now totally changed: she couldn't even recognize the train station. She stopped in front of a florist's and looked at herself in the shining pane of its window. She saw herself grasping her pendant, dressed almost like a teenager, and looked for her face amid flowering orchids and ceramic pots. Her skin shone with perspiration and her long hair fell loose and dry, sticking to her face and shoulders. Her feverish eyes, the brown shadows beneath her eyelids, reminded her that she needed to eat and go to sleep.

All she'd had to eat the day before was a ham sandwich and a bag of toffees she'd bought at the station in Madrid before boarding the train. She was thirsty. She wanted to know what time it was, but wasn't even wearing her watch. She wasn't carrying anything at all. Only the money clasped in her left hand, the pendant, and the keys. She realized her pants had pockets and filled them up, leaving her hands free. She felt more at ease, and started striding out again toward the place where she'd been dying to live for at least a month.

She didn't know why, but she was certain she was going in the right direction.

On the way, she noticed a sign announcing a hairdressing salon and decided to get her hair washed. She waited until she was sure there was nobody awaiting their turn. At the door, she discreetly inspected the place and could only see an empty salon with two sinks for washing hair, each in front of a mirror. The mirrors were oval, with gaudy golden frames and colored stones incrusted in them. The chairs were upholstered in a poor imitation of red velveteen. A young man, wearing his hair in a rusty cock's comb, was filing his nails with extreme care, resting his hands on his knees. He was sitting in front of one of the mirrors, listening to music from a CD through earphones. When he saw her, the young man removed the earphones and adjusted the black peignoir he was wearing over a tight pair of black-and-green tartan pants.

'Good afternoon.'

'I want to get my hair washed.'

The young man felt her hair. It was well taken care of and hydrated. All it needed was for its accumulated dirt to be removed. It hadn't been long since some violet locks were dyed, setting off vibrant reflections in her black hair. When Nuria caught sight of her hair reflected in the mirror, she was surprised by the image of a hair salon similar to that one, and of a woman bending over a head of short blonde hair like a boy's. That unexpected memory took a mere moment to disappear, but the girl felt a flash of floating desire to get her hair cut above ear level and change its color. It occurred to her that she'd worn a style and a cut like that before.

*Before.*

Seated at the sink, she thought about the significance of *before*. For her, time didn't pass in a linear manner and, furthermore, it was something that had substance, as if it were rather like a spherical body that contained her and spurted her out when she needed to advance or grow. It was like a birth every time, the birth of a sphere. And it happened in phases of her life, not in years or months, not in fractions of hours, seconds or minutes. Not even in days or weeks, but as if in a succession of states of consciousness or even in states of animation. She would jump from one to another without transition, without anywhere to lean on. Because of that, she would continuously lose references to time, and sometimes didn't even remember how old she was.

'Bet...' She murmured the name, shaken loose by an inopportune memory. As soon as she realized she was talking aloud, she wriggled around in her chair, trying to recover the tension with which she'd entered. She couldn't allow herself to relax. If she relaxed too much, her head would be spitting out awful things.

'Aren't you comfortable enough?' asked the hairdresser.

'Yes, yes. I was just remembering a friend of mine. I'm sorry, sometimes I talk to myself.'

She remembered herself *before* as a strong, compact woman. That was the image she'd had of herself before she'd accepted Bet as an inevitable part of her life. Previously, several years before that, she was a woman entire. Bet. She thought of her again when the cold water ran down her neck. When it warmed up, she saw the vision of the girl again and felt a rush of happiness. It wasn't that she'd felt happy at that moment, but an imprecise, future intuition of happiness, which had already made itself known while the hairdresser's hands washed her hair. She liked being rubbed on her head, being given massages, especially on the back of her neck. As soon as someone touched the back of her neck, something like a spark would fly.

'Is the water okay?'

'It's perfect,' she answered, making herself comfortable in her chair.

She gave up again, wanting to feel calm. The aroma of vanilla shampoo, the warm water spinning around on the back of her neck, the hairdresser's hands pressing her temples... she stretched her legs, and at last permitted her muscles to become distended and an involuntary smile of satisfaction to appear on her anguish-constricted mouth.

She looked at herself in the mirror before she left. She seemed to have freed herself of an enormous weight. The disappearance of the dirt causing her long hair to sag and sadden allowed her to smile effortlessly. As if her head weighed a lot less. She felt light, even content. Before leaving, she asked the hairdresser what time it was.

It was seven-thirty in the evening.

She didn't know how much she still had to walk to get to the apartment. She had to reach the large beach and, from there, cross a confusion of tall rocks by the sea and a small mountain of pine saplings and eucalyptus trees. Then she would see the cliff protecting a gray, misty area on which the building stood. As she walked, she began to recognize certain things, like the tall rocks jutting out of the sea, and the pines that had survived the two decades of unmanaged construction.

She followed the path that led to an urbanization, where, because of its obscene height and emerald-blue color, the building she was going to live in stood out. She was disillusioned when she saw it... it was horrifying. It actually looked abandoned. Shabby, sad, huge: its beautiful blue was littered with whitened stains, suppurating with rime. The humidity had caused the walls to mark a straight ribbon under the roof in a green tone. Regardless of that, it was there, in the most perfect place. Standing erect above the cliff from which, looking to the right, one could see the mouth of the River Ulla and, to the left, the sparkling reflection of the Arousa estuary.

Six floors of sheer audacity and bad taste, surrounded by interconnected balconies with no interruptions at all.

'I've got it. I'm home already. Now everything's going to go well.' And she said this without believing a word of it, with a smile somewhere between disappointed and excited.

She always got it. She didn't exactly know how it happened, but without planning it she had already inhabited several houses which, years before moving in, had been attractive to her, even eerily familiar. It was as if she'd previously had *visions* of those spaces. It had happened in Lisbon. When she visited the city for the first time, she was fascinated by a pink house with its windows decorated with garlands of white flowers and, as soon as she caught sight of it, she received the impression she had lived there before. Years later, when work brought her to that city, she ended up living in one of its rooms that looked like a cake made of strawberries and cream. The rooms were so familiar to her that she began to feel disquieted by the precision with which she found plugs, holes in the furniture, and marks on the walls. She even recognized the sweetened scent of cigarettes smoked by one of the tenants, which was mixed with the wax used to polish the wooden floors and the dark, antique furniture. It was an uncommon sensation of familiarity. It had occurred in several other houses, in apartments and cities where she'd lived, sometimes because of her work, and others, as on this occasion, by the overbearing need to start again, to change. To change her life so she could continue to be unalterable. Unique.

‘It may be that I’ve lived other lives, that I do live other lives.’ She’d laugh as she told the stories of her houses. ‘Or perhaps I’m a thousand persons living in several places at the same time.’

‘Or perhaps unconsciously, once you’ve seen them, it’s you who look out for them.’ She always found someone who brought sense back to her. ‘It’s the most logical thing, right?’

‘I don’t know. Maybe. I like to think there’s something I’m unable to control, that there’s something mysterious about this whole thing...’

But she really had chosen the cliff apartment. She’d decided on it years ago. It was on an afternoon when, lying on the sand, her body smelling of sex and salt, she longed with all her strength to live at the top of the building under construction. At the highest spot. When she received the call from that Xoaquín Cuns and decided to take a vacation, she thought of it as a refuge where she could start anew. It would be a good place to come together as one and flee from dispersion. She had an intuition that for her, such a change would feel like something similar to starting a flight on a plane, when the land pulled down everything undesirable, and she moved immaculately towards the clouds, free of all burdens. Towards herself... cleansed. Or perhaps she might even stay in the apartment forever, and change life into permanent vacations with views of the sea. And she would draw again. Although her work in recent years was almost completely limited to designing floral motifs for a ceramics factory in Lisbon, she was convinced that at the same time as she became whole again, she would be possessed by an unusual creative force. She would paint as before, unique ideas would occur to her. She wouldn't think of suicide all the time, and would move away from that repetitive image as if it were already engraved in her retina, in which she hung from a rope while grasping a revolver in each hand. That brutal image, whose birth within her was unknown, would at last disappear.

She walked through the center of the urbanization, following the path that led to the top of the cliff. The asphalt was swollen and stuck together, and herbs and brambles were beginning to grow on the sidewalks. Some of the small, single-family houses remained closed or totally abandoned, their gardens filled with brambles. Despite the evident neglect and deterioration, there was a supermarket and a couple of open bars. Outside one of the bars some youngsters, each seated in a chair on the sidewalk, were drinking beer and chatting while music played from a radio cassette in the background. It smelled of the sea and summer, in a mixture of rime and tanning lotion, fried fish and salads. Boys and girls were playing in the low-walled gardens, and dogs, suffocating in the heat, slept in the shadows of the houses and pines. Shells from the beach were scattered over the asphalt, crunching underfoot when they were stepped on and broken.

Anxiously, she took to the path again, sweating, and shoved the key into her pants pocket. She didn't recall that coastline rising up because when she used to go swimming in the bay, it was only possible to get to the top by clambering like a cat over the stones. And it turned out to be too difficult, because the abrupt cliff must have been about four or five meters high and invariably thronged with seagulls. During the rough climb she bumped into a girl dressed in a short, yellow summer pinafore dress, turning around and around and doing herself harm. The girl repeated endlessly, 'I'm a monk and I'm also a monkey.'

She knew that game, thought of the word 'monkey,' and repeated it mentally, depriving it of its significance until the syllables were floating in a hole formed in her brain. The monkey ended up turning into a monk, with the impressive naturalness with which the girl kept turning around without becoming nauseated. Without trying to, she thought of Bet again, and how diffuse the limits could be between the two of them. At times they seemed too much like each other but, actually, they were two absolutely different people. All the same, if she had wished to do so, she could have made Bet look like herself. But she didn't want to. She avoided the dangerous temptation to call her and faced the final meters (more pines than before) to enter the tree-filled garden in front of the building. Previously, she'd turned around to look at the girl again. She looked familiar, as if she'd always been with her, but she'd never focused on her until that moment.

In the garden the pines and some eucalyptus trees had grown so tall they cast shadows on the building. Under the trees, in spaces shut off by low stone walls and iron bars, she could almost discern steel benches and a small lake which at one time must have welcomed ducks and swans. There were rhododendron and hydrangea bushes, a few neglected rose bushes, and a flight of steps adorned with tiles showing dolphins and fishes in blue tones. The steps led to the entrance of the building, where, above the door, she could see the name Seabeach.

On the lowest floor of the building, to the left of the entrance and with views of the estuary, there was a restaurant with a terrace that looked out onto the beach, and Nuria, before inserting the key in the portal, looked furtively at the views and was absolutely delighted to be there. She heard hunger growling in her stomach, but was so keen to go up to her apartment and lean on the balcony she decided to leave dinner for later.

The entrance surprised her. It was as scary as the building itself: a huge rectangular space opened up before a solitary stone cabinet, a pretentious staircase that imitated marble, and two golden elevators. The floor was covered in large white tiles that also replicated marble, and which continued with the representation of dolphins and fishes in bright blue colors and gold. Several ficus plants were leaning on one of the walls, worn out by age and neglect, covering the mail-boxes with their undernourished leaves. Nuria, ahead of the possible deception she would suffer as she entered the apartment, repeated to herself that the *visions* had only shown her the sunsets and the sea: the sunsets red, and the sea reflecting everything, as does a dolphin's back.

She took the elevator to the fifth floor. The elevator was silent, and it was just as silent when it stopped, and as gentle. It opened onto a new, copious space, also with marble tiles with dolphins and fishes, and the walls painted blue, like the paintwork outside.

And also, like the building seen from the exterior, it had dark stains and suppurations whitened by salt. It smelled musty and fungus-ridden. That smell reminded her of a damp, lumpy cocaine she would take from time to time, and she instinctively put her fingers on the windows and began to breathe.

Six apartments opened onto the corridor. She knew without a shadow of doubt which was hers, and stopped immediately in front of door 5E. It was a humdrum door, fragile, made of dark wood. It would open at a simple kick. But solemnly, Nuria inserted the key and turned it, listening for any sounds. A dry creak, a single turn, and the door opened. She could have entered, but waited for a moment, to listen with her eyes shut. And suddenly she heard the sound of the sea. A sweet, almost nauseating smell of raw meat, warm blood, and orange blossoms. The heaviness of the heat was suffocating, and, even with her eyes closed, she seemed to hear someone within herself pronouncing her name: Nuria. She heard it clearly: Nuria. She supposed it was the anxiety to know the reason for that type of auditory hallucination. Or hunger. She opened her eyes and fell back. The total darkness forced her to leave the apartment and invade the corridor, pushing her there. A blast of hot air, as if it had been compressed for months, obliged her to go back a few steps while the door opened and she was shown a roomy waiting area with a china cabinet against the wall, a sight that became clearer at every moment. Above the china cabinet was a rectangular sticker from something that had been hanging there at some point. Next to it was a set of hangers with paintings of reproductions of those romantic postcards showing couples kissing amid rose bushes, or against unreal sunsets.

Once inside, she ventured to test the previous *visions*. With slight variations, everything was where she *knew* it ought to be. There had to be five doors: one for the bathroom, one for the large room, one for the small room, one for the kitchen and one for the living room. And there were five doors. She opened them and raised the blinds. The raw red light from the sunset shook the apartment, which awoke like a mass of living flesh that had received the breath of life. Nuria, at last leaning forward on her elbows on the railing of the balcony, convinced herself she'd made the right decision: just by living for a time encircled by that almost scarlet light, by the narcotic rumor of the waves, and by the spicy fragrance of the salt and the pine trees, she had made the right decision.

And there she spent hours, and there she fell asleep, without being bothered by hunger pangs, or the fact that – despite all her efforts to arrive at the apartment cleansed of anything having to do with her life before she boarded a train in Madrid – she carried on her body Bet's redolence and the kiss that Tomás Induvina gave her when they said goodbye.

And the pendant hanging from her neck.

# 5

It occurred to the tiny little thing within that space, which could have been a nutshell or a space station, that she should think with her sex and breasts – but what would sex and breasts be? – and feel with her head – and what would the head be?

Later, the little creature asked herself:

'What is thinking? What is feeling?'

Bet was dreaming. In the dream she was searching for a place to thrust through to the light, though she didn't know exactly where it was. She knew, for a fact, that she had to wait.

# 6

The conductor of the school bus helped the children board and gave them each a cookie shaped like a heart. Greedy-guts that they were, they ate them up before they sat down, still in a confusion of knapsacks and coats. When all the children were inside, the driver, an amiable man, made sure they were all in their seats. After that, he got the bus going. He guided it through the streets of the city, and finally turned onto a country road and stopped in a wooded area of mixed, large trees. All the kids were asleep, dreaming of sweet, red hearts, like their cookies. The driver headed down the bus and, having made sure the children were fast asleep, lifted them and hung them by their feet from butcher-style hooks on the roof. He went from row to row, and the children hung head-down, their falling arms brushing the seats. But one child hadn't eaten his cookie, and, sheltered among the seats, watched what was happening in a hypnotic state. Until suddenly he, too, was hanging from a hook.

With the children hanging from the roof, the driver took a sword from the net supporting the luggage. Brandishing it expertly, he cut off heads as if they were flowers in a field. Blood gushed. From the blood spilled on the ground, there arose landscapes, the landscapes the children had seen or dreamed of. A landscape for each child. Just to see that, it was worth the lad who hadn't eaten his cookie hanging with blood beating down his temples, increasingly beset by fear. To see the children's dreams materializing on the rug on the bus floor, it was worth hanging head down and feeling his panic interfere with his breathing, preventing him from screaming. He allowed it to happen, and watched like a spectator until the sword shone brilliantly before him and death scratched at his throat. He forgot that his feet were tied. Then he opened his eyes as wide as he could, smiled, did his best to perform an acrobatic leap, got covered in filth, but it didn't work. He forgot his feet were tied and he was hanging from the roof. The murderer's expression sparkled, and now tender, he doubled over with the intention of also hanging his head face down, and had the kindness to say to the boy:

'Ha ha, don't be afraid, Tomás. It's going to be quick, very quick.'

And it *was* quick: he sliced off the boy's head with one true, precise blow. Just as his head was about fall to the ground like the heads of the other children, Tomás

Induvina landed on his bed with a jump and touched his neck with his hand. He was breathing with difficulty, his lungs were painful and weak, losing strength from so much smoking. He felt nauseous and leapt up, compelled by the need to vomit.

In the bathroom, leaning over the sink and with his mouth filthy with the remains of the vomit, he looked at himself in the mirror trying to remember what he'd done the previous night. What had he been drinking? What had he put in his body to dream such a thing? Children being decapitated like lambs. The image of some daffodils he'd discovered in a poem came to his mind. There also came to his mind the image of President George Washington whittling his teeth on a wooden denture. He couldn't understand a thing. He washed his face, rinsed his mouth, and walked around the studio in search of answers.

Tomás Induvina was a painter. A painter of the great formats of the full figurative explosion of the eighties. He was obsessed with the sea and with white walls. He painted enormous, colorful white walls. He said that white was full of delicate changes that could go from white itself to black, the medium covering the entire chromatic spectrum, and, because of this, his paintings of white walls, full of color, had brought him quite a lot of success, and had been lucrative at the beginning of the decade. The painting of the sea was of his mother's seaside village, on the Coast of Death.

He lived in Madrid, where he'd moved to find a path for himself. For a while he'd managed a certain success, but, lonely and with periodic creative crises, he'd had to accept in order to survive a series of jobs decorating nightclubs and clothing stores. He owned a studio where he also lived: an old warehouse that had dealt in iron goods, and still contained the remains of iron and a penetrating odor of rust and rancid oil. It was outside Madrid, in the great avenue where the traffic from the north blended with the capital. It was quite noisy, but very well lit.

At an almost catastrophic moment, a girl calling herself Bet appeared at the studio. She came on behalf of a mutual friend, but Induvina never knew who he was. Bet needed a place to work and sleep for some months. She was a woman of about twenty-odd years, fleeing from some uncertain place and from a situation she never mentioned, and had offered to pay him sufficiently, so Induvina accepted her as a lodger. In time, without meaning to, he began to fall in love with that girl, who, surprisingly, turned up to sleep, would disappear and appear again, spending hours designing performances in which she was her own act. They discussed art quite a lot; she'd say her body was the object, the content, and the finality of her creation. Little by little, and at the same rhythm that Induvina fell in love with her, Bet brought to the studio tubes of oil paint that she filched from stores, magazines, books – and huge piles of projects that were almost never finished, either because they bored her or she'd simply disappear.

Induvina was about forty. He was tall, strong, and attractive. He'd inherited from his mother inquisitive blue eyes and brown hair, which he usually wore long and tied back in a ponytail. Bet was attracted by his tendency to depression, his readings of psychedelic authors, and the affection they shared in consuming all kinds of drugs. But perhaps what Bet liked most was the facility with which she could manipulate him, even to the point of cruelty. She'd managed to make Induvina's life one of hanging onto her every wish, in a state of permanent alert.

Animated by his companion's creativity, he began to paint again. He recovered his energy and shared his ideas with her, which at first Bet applauded and encouraged. Those were splendid months for Induvina, when he was even vivacious enough to leave his studio and display his exhibits again. Even so, there were times when Bet hammered him mercilessly, insisting he would never be successful if he continued painting that way, and when they argued, she never missed a chance to tell him he was a failure.

But Induvina, against Bet's expectations, wasn't afraid of failure. Failure, when it came down to it, was something final, definitive, and easy to live with. What he couldn't put up with was mediocrity, of which his work (like so many works of art) formed part, like a din of voices, all of them the same.

'To distinguish yourself you'll have to do something different,' she responded challengingly.

'I already do that.'

'No, no you don't. You *paint*.' And she said this to him disparagingly, and he looked at her with his mouth open in surprise, in humiliation, expecting something more – words that would comfort him and were never spoken.

That was part of the cruelty of the girl. She ignored the basic rules of courtesy and diplomacy and would say what for her no doubt was pure clairvoyance. At times, that absolute, egotistical clairvoyance sounded like a drunken outburst of superiority and disdain, terrifying everyone who heard it.

But Bet was like that, and that was why he loved her.

A great deal of light came in through the windows of the studio, through the enormous windows that started at the floor and went up to the roof. Some three meters' height and ten meters of adobe and glass façade. The light seemed heavy, as if made of a solid material. The odor of rust was mixed with a strong whiff of tar and turpentine. It smelled a little of the sea, perhaps from the tar he was working with on two large canvasses that covered the walls. The light hurt his eyes and his face. It pierced them. He realized he was naked and backed away from the window, more because of the pain of the glare in his eyes than the fear that someone would see him in the altogether.

The noise of the traffic gave him a headache. He searched for analgesics and a bottle of beer to soothe the dryness of his mouth and the acidity of the alcohol and cigarettes. He passed in front of the canvasses, deprived of a frame and sustained by being nailed to the wall. On a big metal table, covered with papers and boxes of paintings, he found traces of the previous night: an empty bottle of whisky, a plate covered in cigarette butts and ash, some leftovers of cocaine, a blood-stained, impossibly-crumpled thousand-peseta bill, and a scrap of aluminum foil with the remnants of a brown, burned substance. The table was illuminated by the light of a lantern covered in transparent uralite. Little by little, so that it wouldn't hurt him, a memory began to develop: Bet. He was attacked by that physical pain that came to him whenever Bet went away. It would start in his intestines, prevent him from eating, and knock him flat out in bed for days. As if a small part of his body had been yanked out. He felt her absence like a heady, persistent pain submerging him into a state of desolation and apathy.

He moved to the back part of the warehouse, which was half in penumbra, illuminated solely by the light filtering through the lantern. There, behind a black, plastic curtain hanging from the roof, was the part of the studio occupied by Bet. He'd hoped to find her there, at work. But she wasn't. Seeing her red-leather jacket abandoned on the floor gave him a fit of horror-stricken trembling. He picked it up, gave its silver studs another rubbing, and laid it on an old leatherette sofa that Bet called 'the thinking sofa.' Parallel to the sofa he saw a sculpture that always made him feel horribly uncomfortable: above a steel closet were some rusty butcher's hooks; hanging from the hooks, in unpolluted white, was a line of babies' corpses, apparently sweetly asleep. The work of Carlos Rial, a friend of Bet's that Induvina had never met. Bet liked having it there, she'd say it caused her a commotion, that it aroused her. But for Induvina it was painful. Perhaps because behind that pain his jealousies were showing. But they weren't jealousies that had anything to do with affection, like the fear of her being in love with the sculptor. No – he was jealous of what Carlos's work had awakened in Bet. Jealous of that *commotion* that none of his own works had produced in her.

On the wall, in an unfinished mural, a single photograph was reproduced a thousand times in different colors, imitating a kind of old-fashioned, bloody, apocalyptic ark. The face in the photograph imitated Bet's, but wasn't Bet. It had an expression he'd never seen on her before. Sweeter, ingenuous, that of a pure girl. Without a touch of malevolence. Untouched. Innocent, perhaps. Maybe she'd looked like that before she met Induvina, but he doubted it. It wasn't her, but perhaps she had wanted to be that young girl in the photograph.

Initially, the photograph was a black-and-white close-up of a face with large eyes, full of life, the lines of the nose diluted by the paleness of the face. The lips, half-open in a transparent smile that showed her teeth, small but well-aligned, without malice. With no predatory desires. Although the profile of the face looked like Bet's, the hair was different, short and blonde like a boy's. That photograph, reproduced in all imaginable colors in the mural on the wall, had been treated by the computer on the table, which remained turned off, revealing her absence. He'd seen the evolution of that work. He'd seen, as well, how Bet had evolved day by day, at the same rate that the mural was growing. Until she wanted to leave, until she finally left.

'*Ciao, ciao, bambina,*' he sang softly, after he'd blown a kiss to the girl in the photo.

He continued for a while in her part of the studio, stopping to look at things in which he had previously shown no interest: *Judith Beheading Holofernes*, by Artemisa Gentileschi, struck him as particularly bloodthirsty at that time, perhaps unnecessarily cruel. There were several photographs of works by Ana Mendieta stuck with staples onto a cork board, and representations of saints with mutilated bodies. From the roof hung jellyfish created from the most diverse papers, from pages of journals to pieces of painted paper, and, together with the jellyfish, tied with fishing lines and beams, there dangled dozens of baguettes she had painted as if they were goldfish. Piled on the desk were collages, books on art and feminism, brochures discussing exhibitions, notes on possible performances, and plaster of Paris heads of dolls. Accidentally, he came across a folder of geometric and floral designs with a very clear signature: Nuria Uría. The writing was small, compact, and neat, but timorous and diffident – very different from Bet's handwriting, which came in large, furious, confident flourishes, though at times it was almost illegible.

Induvina didn't know who Nuria was. Bet had never spoken about her to him. Or had she? He recalled a day when she said she'd like him to meet someone – a friend. That friend might have been her, Nuria. She was a debutante, or a designer, or...

'Yes, it must be her. She worked in Portugal.' The discovery at the head of the papers with the drawings of the name of a Lisbon ceramics factory confirmed this, and he stopped thinking about her.

He placed the folder on the table and looked through the house for sleeping pills. He didn't find any. On his glass table, next to the empty bottle of whisky, he discovered a small wrapping with a little pinch of heroin in it. He picked up a scrap of aluminum foil and threw the wrapping into it. He waited for a while before he moved the wrapping up to the lighter flame, in case the telephone or the door-bell rang. While he was waiting, he downed the little whisky that was left at the bottom of the glass. Nothing happened. Not even the babies hanging from the butcher's hooks emitted a redeeming sound. In the end he lit the *chino* and absorbed the narcotic smoke. He walked unsteadily to the bed and let himself fall into the tangle of sheets.

He was sweating. Thirty-six degrees in Madrid at one in the afternoon. That was the time when Induvina lay down, befuddled by the steam from the drug. Before he became soporific, his mind recited a poem about a field of daffodils, and saw President George Washington pulling out the teeth of the children decapitated by the bus conductor. He felt as if his own head were falling to the ground, and knew that he was seeing the world from the linoleum at the foot of the bed. He tried to move, but weighed so much that, just as he was getting up, he let himself be taken to the depths of a dark, dry dream.

# 7

That first morning she was awoken by the clamor of seagulls and, perturbed by the presence of the birds poised on the railing of the balcony, she got up. She was surprised at their size and the whiteness of their feathers. She looked at them from behind the glass, without getting close. The birds soon left, flying towards the pier. She was hungry, her stomach ached, and her empty innards emitted scandalous roars. She had been so tired the previous night that she'd gone to bed without dinner and slept deeply, without changing her position. She didn't dream of anything, and had no anxieties.

Before she showered and went down to breakfast, she decided to make sure she had everything she needed in the apartment, and started to walk through the rooms.

The apartment was a large square, in which two sides – the ones opening out onto the continuous balcony side by side – were covered by large glass sliding doors. She had light available all day long. From every corner one could see the open estuary facing the ocean, the mountains and the town that clawed like a cat up the mountainsides that were a mixture of pines and oaks. She had the necessary items: a bed and a chest of drawers in the room, sheets, blankets, and a pair of worn-out but clean towels. A table with four chairs occupied the center of the living room, where there was a sofa upholstered in bottle-green material and a television on a little glass table. In the kitchen she found a few items of crockery, some cutlery with yellow plastic handles that didn't match, half-a dozen glasses, and a pair of bowls. Briefly, all you needed for a short vacation.

As she got into the shower she remembered she didn't have any soap, gel, or toothpaste. Or a brush or comb. She washed herself entirely with water, and afterwards, on looking for a mirror at which to comb her hair, she discovered there wasn't a single one anywhere in the house. There wasn't even a mirror in the little white metal cupboard in the bathroom. In the corridor, over the china cabinet at the entrance, there was the mark of something that had been hung there, and, scattered over it almost like litter, she discovered tiny shards of glass.

She decided she had to buy one. She wanted to see the evolution of her body and her face as the days passed. Her intention to reunify herself, to be just one person, demanded strict attention to her body. No drugs, no toxic food. She would swim, run until exhausted, until her muscles turned into hard flesh, until she fell into bed at night worn out and satisfied. That was what she wanted.

'Toothpaste, brush, comb, mirror...' she repeated to herself as she waited for the elevator to go down to the restaurant. 'Toothpaste and underwear.'

Suddenly she spotted a small, round woman in front of the door to one of the apartments. From her neck to her knees, the woman was a bulging body, without a waist or hips. She was wearing a Lycra swimsuit, which clung obscenely to the cracks in her compacted flesh. This called attention to her wrinkles, her breasts, and her crotch. It was a diffuse color that went from blue to green to yellow, according to the light. As the woman moved, bright lights like water stains would extend or disappear.

'Will you be going down, madam?' asked Nuria amiably.

But the woman didn't answer, apparently paying attention to some children who were laughing inside one of the apartments. Nuria pressed the button. The elevator stopped in the reception area and opened its door to that solitude of dying ficus plants on the marble tiles. She left, rapidly crossing the tiled floor to the restaurant, mystified by hunger and repeating:

'Mirror, toothbrush, comb, and a swimsuit. A black swimsuit.'

She had a good appetite for lunch as she surveyed the sea. She recognized the terrace, still solitary, still in shadow, like the phrase of an ancient song she recalled in fragments. The tables and chairs, repainted a thousand times in white, gave a healthy varnish to that first August morning, following the decadent texture of the dolphins and the blue fishes that, also present, were scattered over the floor. She had moved like a patient to a spa, to a rest clinic, to a retirement home, where the obligation to remain passive and accept the care of others was presented to her like a delightful occasion to surrender to laziness. To surrender to laziness, to passivity, to the pleasure of inertia.

'Good morning,' said an old man who sat down at the next table to read the newspaper. He was wearing sunglasses and a white canvas hat.

Smiling complicitly as he greeted her, he waited for a while, expecting something from Nuria, something more than the brusque 'good morning' she had bestowed upon him. But she wanted to be alone and furthermore, that man, for some reason, disgusted her. She stood up and went over to the stone wall bordering the terrace. She noticed its height: some five meters from the sand on the beach. The old-style door, also made of wood with a white paint job like the tables and chairs, opened up to some little steps carved into the stone that reached the edge of the sea.

On her way back to the apartment she picked up an envelope at the mailbox. She knew what it contained, because she herself had sent it when she was sure she would be moving there. She opened the envelope while she took the elevator upstairs, to make sure everything was inside: her identity document, the credit card, and a photograph. She took out the identity document and the bank card and found space for them in her pants pocket. The envelope with the photograph inside, she placed on the china cabinet almost with disdain.

She went into the kitchen, attracted by the light reflected by the granite countertops. It was small, narrow, and ended in a glass door that opened onto the balcony. She let herself be caressed by the light and by a gentle breeze bringing in the warmth of the south. She had the impression she'd forgotten something, that there was something she needed to resolve. It was something that made her uncomfortable, just as she was made uncomfortable by the unusual certainty that she would never gain anything by being absolutely alone, as if there were many people inside her, inhabiting her, making noise. Perhaps that was why she was always so tired. Because she didn't know what it was like to be really alone. Or what perfect solitude was.

Two crows flew in from the stony hillside visible from beyond the urbanization, and perched on the crown of a eucalyptus. They remained in its branches, grooming themselves with their beaks, and then became still, half stupefied. The morning breeze vibrated on their black, shining feathers, and Nuria enjoyed that moment of calm. The crows ensnared her in their flight and kept her caught up in the blue-toned blackness of their plumage. Hypnotized by them, she felt like an outsider until she heard the voices of some children who seemed to be playing in the living room. Together with the children's voices she heard a woman begging them to be quiet. The crows flew away, and alarmed, she entered the apartment. There was nobody there, and the voices fell silent. Perhaps it was the apartment next door where the voices had come from. Perhaps there'd been a family with children there. Perhaps it was the woman in the swimsuit she'd seen when she'd gone down for lunch. Perhaps. It would be inevitable – if there was indeed a family living on the same floor – that they would see each other. Even if they avoided it, it would be very easy to bump into each other on the balcony, because the apartments' balconies were only separated by modest iron filigree work that didn't permit any kind of intimacy.

*But the voices.* There were moments when she seemed to hear ancient voices, words pronounced in another time, perhaps in another time sphere.

On the parquet over the corridor floor she then came across some stains she'd never noticed before. They were brown stains that oozed an oily humidity, and looked like barefoot stickers. The footsteps were all over the wooden floor, from the main door to the living room balcony. Looking at them, she felt an urgent need to purchase cleaning products. She sensed it was her duty to give those stains a good scrubbing and to go over the whole apartment – although, from what she could see, it was clean. Too clean for what would be expected of a place that had been uninhabited for some time. But maybe the real estate agency had tidied it up before she arrived. She remembered the musty odor that had overcome her the previous night, when she opened the door and doubted whether anyone had entered the apartment for weeks or months. She laughed at her ingenuity in thinking that the people from the agency were in charge of doing the cleaning. She didn't pay any further importance to it and went downstairs, having decided to do her shopping in the supermarket she'd seen at the entrance to the urbanization. She calculated how much money she had in her pockets and discovered that she had enough to buy what she needed. Clothes, too. Above all, she had to purchase underwear and a swimsuit.

When she left the portal and crossed the little tree-decorated garden that gave access to the building, she'd foreseen that at least on that first day, fragments of ancient memories would come into her head from the time she'd spent in the town, because she'd lived there for two years as a teenager, when her father was sent to work on the reconstruction of the piers in the mid-seventies. His leaving and the total disintegration of the family were precipitated by events that Nuria couldn't remember, and which were not mentioned by any member of the family either. In spite of everything, Nuria knew that at least she hadn't lived through those years with indifference. Her intuition told her they'd been intense. But she didn't remember them. One of the problems with her anomalous perception of time was the facility with which the memories were diluted in that elastic, physical substance in which her life transpired.

But the worst wasn't forgetfulness, it was the fact they'd attributed exploits to her of which she was only remotely conscious. In fact, there were women among her friends who had stopped talking to her, who had fled from her, and, when asked the reason for this, would respond that she, Nuria, was a bad person.

'You have terrible manners. Do you know what you said yesterday, Nuria?' asked a friend (whom she never saw again) to her face. 'You said something like "There are beings like you who think in ways that advance humanity" and, later on, that "We are the poor folk who can't even serve to procreate." What kind of a nutcase are you?'

Nuria was left disconcerted, because she considered herself a shy, loving, understanding woman. She wanted to be the best person in the world, and treated people with delicacy. She took great care to do nice things with her women friends, hugging them when they were sad, giving them presents. But even so, little by little Nuria was becoming lonely without knowing why. And that wasn't exactly the loneliness she felt so much longing for.

She tried to remember the life of those two years of adolescence in the town, and got the impression of intensity, of density. She thought that if she were a tree that had been cut into slices, the corresponding rings would be of greater consistency than the rest: more compact, and they would give off a different color and fragrance. But, despite their being intense, she barely preserved any fragments of emotions and some imprecise images that manifested themselves to her, especially during the bizarre nightmares that often woke her up awash in sweat. She always *knew* that at some moment something very dangerous would happen to her there. And that knowledge came to her, made softer by an excessively sweetened taste of kisses and caresses and sex, and from the touch of hot sand on her skin. From the touch of another body about which all she could say was that its skin was vibrant, made tense by the urgency of its desire like the leather on a drum. A new skin, that still smelled of children's cologne, chocolate, and orange juice.

Those scraped-down, imprecise memories that opened an unexpected path for themselves, snatched reality from her regardless of where she was. It might happen as she walked along a street, as it did at that moment. Then she fell silent, stammered, and looked around in case someone else had noticed the atrocity that had rendered her limping and paralyzed. One day it was an image, another, a conversation, another, a sharp pain in some part of her body. It was always something unspecific and disquieting, such as that uncomfortable sensation of having something pending, or that other feeling of always having someone with her. She put her hand to her lips, where she'd felt the contact of an inexpert mouth, the fresh, mixed saliva of a timid but voracious mouth. She was startled and left the garden in a hurry, wanting to flee from that temporal sphere, jumping onto it to get into another one, hopefully kinder and more luminous. But, in reality – as she knew very well – everything was reduced to that elastic, present time that had lasted since she got off the train. There was nothing beyond the train, only spheres scattered by her existence like those large islands that appeared in the estuary at low tide. Nothing that wasn't a pile of chaotic memories. Diluted borders. Images burnt by the side of the road. That was the past, something as distant as the cave inhabited by an Australopithecus four million years before she herself was there. She remembered (and did not pretend to find) a logical explanation for that memory: she was lying in pile of leaves and branches, fondling a baby that was biting her breasts as it sucked at them. That's how that strange memory began and ended. She didn't know why, but she also recognized having passed over desert sand extending to the foot of some red mountains, and that memory brought peace, and stimulated something in her brain that, as well as peace, gave her happiness and caused her mouth to spill with the sweet, fresh taste of a red fruit.

Bemused, she was almost run over by a boy on his bike. He asked to be forgiven, and continued pedaling and marking the route she should follow to leave the urbanization. She crossed in front of a man who looked familiar, but, before she became alarmed, she realized he was the old man who had greeted her that morning in the restaurant. She felt again that there was something in him she seemed familiar with from *before*. *Before*. He was a thin, gaunt man whose hair was entirely white, though thick. She guessed he must be about seventy from the wrinkles on his face, and because he walked as if he were half mangled, like an old dog with broken-down hips. He was wearing white linen, with leather sandals and a navy-blue silk scarf. He carried a camera on his shoulder.

'Have you moved in already?' he asked her, looking at her again as if he were expecting some sign of proximity from her.

But Nuria didn't answer. She continued walking without looking back, her head down and her arms crossed over her stomach, pressing it, trying to protect herself.

'I don't know who they are, I don't know who they are,' she repeated in a voice loud enough for the boy on the bike to turn his head and look curiously at her.

In the supermarket at the urbanization there was everything she needed. An obese woman with very black hair gathered up in a green headscarf attended the cash register. Her face was round, red, and happy. She seemed sweetly familiar.

'So you've come back this year?' asked the woman, trying to be pleasant, but as Nuria didn't answer, she looked her up and down and asked to be pardoned. 'I took you for somebody else.'

Nuria didn't flinch. She'd also thought that the waitress attending the restaurant looked at her as if she knew her from somewhere, just like the old man with whom she'd crossed the street. 'Coincidences,' she thought, and asked where there might be a haberdashery.

'About half an hour away, as you pass the beach.'

She set off walking, tempted to continue on to the town to buy nice clothes, but decided to spend that first day in the apartment. To become familiar with it, to pay attention to the noises in order to avoid disagreeable surprises, such as murmurs, voices, footsteps, creaks, or the dying breaths of people she didn't know. She should get to know all the textures of the new house, the nuances of the light, the changes in temperature, the sound of the water pipes and the gas. The possible tricks of the electricity. It was fundamental to know the space well, so that nothing would get in the way of her reunification. She didn't want any distractions: nothing that for lack of knowledge would make her doubt herself.

She'd fled from a place where something as simple as the disappearance of a pencil had become a nightmare. She remembered with anguish the times she'd arrived home and never known what she was going to find: the gas turned on, a faucet running, clothes thrown on the floor, scraps of food she would never eat. She came from a place where even her breathing would unleash situations of panic. In the beach apartment she was looking for a way to be in control of everything, including herself. She wasn't going to admit any lack of attention, she even had to familiarize herself with the flight of flies and the sound of leaves rustled by the breeze. That was why she was there: to avoid instability. Instability implied another repetition. Steps in the wrong direction. Her unnecessary obligation to control herself more than she already did. The reiteration of words that had stopped signifying something concrete echoed, though diluted, against the walls of her cranium. Empty words, divested of substance: 'I'm a monk, I'm a monkey.' And, in the end, the inevitable question: 'Who am I?' Because of this, she ought to shop for items she couldn't do without, especially cleaning products, and return to the apartment as soon as she could. She had to chew on it, listen carefully to her body until she found the most subtle murmurs, sniff them to detect any scent that didn't proceed from herself, and identify it. She had to return.

With the fixed idea of cleaning up the stains on the parquet, she was disillusioned to discover there were no longer any traces of the greasy footprints she'd seen before leaving the apartment. It also depended on how the sunbeams landed in the corridor. She might have exaggerated, and they weren't really so evident. She didn't give it any more importance, but she scrubbed the wooden floor again and cleaned everything room by room. When she finished, she hung up her new clothes in the closet and put the food carefully into the refrigerator and the pantry. Having completed the work, she prepared a nut-and-tomato salad and ate it on the balcony, in the area of the kitchen where, since midday, the sun hadn't shone. Then she lay down and, stretched out on the bed, and just as she was about to fall into the siesta she was used to, she devoted herself to listening. But, soothed by that supreme sound – the pounding of the waves against the rocks on the cliff – she fell asleep.

At nightfall, following an intense exploration of the apartment, she was exhausted. She managed to soothe somewhat the anxiety with which she'd entered the town the previous afternoon, but it reappeared: perhaps owing to such a precipitated change, being *there* at last. She looked out onto the balcony, listening cautiously. She looked fearfully at the scenery, listening to her body reacting to it. Everything was in its place: the trees, the people on the beach, the water, even the clouds had consistency and were real. They weren't the sort of projections (she called them *holograms*) she sometimes saw and was so afraid of, because they announced changes for which she wasn't always prepared. But no, everything was in order out there, and, therefore, everything was going well inside her head.

She decided to have dinner.

She went down in the elevator and, on arriving at the reception area, she was on the verge of opening the door when she heard a dry shout. It was a woman's shout. Desperately, the elevator kept falling and falling from the height of the building until, after an opaque bump, it hit the tiles – an opaque but humid bump, a splintering of bones that lessened a blow to flesh and blood. She was certain a woman had just leapt from a balcony. She didn't know why, but she was certain. She could also have sworn that the woman was dressed in a Lycra swimsuit and had just thrown herself off the fifth floor balcony, from her apartment. She left, terrified of finding her in pieces from having plummeted onto the terrace, but there was no sign of her. No cadaver. No muddle of blood on the dolphins. Perhaps it had occurred at the other side of the building, the part that faced the beach. She ran to the restaurant terrace, informed the waitress, looked at the wall, and was surprised to see that everything was peaceful. There wasn't a corpse in fragments there either, and people were enjoying the evening's final hour on the little beach.

In a decided tone, Nuria questioned the waitress. Seeing she was so nervous, the woman looked at her condescendingly.

'Calm down. It's the seagulls. Seagulls scream like human beings.'

'I heard a woman.'

'They're like women, like children, swearing like the condemned.'

'I don't know, to tell the truth...'

'Once you get used to them you won't hear them anymore. Just be calm and relaxed...'

'I know, it's the seagulls.'

'So what else would they be?'

'A woman throwing herself off a balcony.'

'Seagulls. Listen to what I say and enjoy the holidays.'

The waitress guided her directly to a table by a window. And seated at the table from that day onward and without requesting it, Nuria saw the man in the fancy blue silk scarf on the terrace, at the same place where that very morning he'd settled down to read the paper. But this time, instead of reading the paper, he was sketching on a ruled pad. He raised his eyes, observed his surroundings, and later, during much more time than he'd invested in observing, he returned to sketching. She didn't like him sketching. That hadn't been the first disagreeable emotion she'd felt since he'd arrived, but it surprised her because it wasn't just any emotion: she sensed the hatred growing in her. If she knew anything about that old, boxed-in man it was that *he shouldn't have been there*.

She finished her dinner and paid at the bar. As she waited for the bill, she noticed the first page of a newspaper: Saturday, March 1st, 1992. *Two aeroplane accidents in Nepal and China. The Barcelona Olympics.* On the front page, above the headline, was a portrait of herself in pencil, drawn with a firm pulse. The long hair, the sad face, the upper lip consumed almost to the point of disappearance, the eyes a deep line on the brow, showing a similarly deep resentment. She became angry when she recognized herself. She was not like that, couldn't be like that: it was impossible! When Nuria paid, the waitress told her Vidal had drawn it – the old man from the terrace. She hated him intensely.

At the elevator mirror she discovered, to her sorrow, the face she'd seen drawn in the newspaper, so different from the image she wanted to show others of herself during that time of re-encounter with the light.

# 8

She walked slowly, surrounded by moths and the distant croaking of frogs. She was walking through a ruinous landscape of dead volcanoes and solidified black lava. Her unshod feet lifted the dust of the esplanade that opened up before her, covered by the darkness of the night. She was half naked, her stomach and breasts nude, though she covered her head with a cloth of white gauze. There was something both sensual and at the same time repulsive in that woman, because her desire was too evident and left in her wake an intense genital odor. In her hands she carried a scythe that gave off a brilliance like rusty iron. As she passed by, the dogs, excited by the woman's odor, howled like wolves in heat, but she wasn't afraid of them, not even looking in a different direction from the path that was dragging her along. At last, still surrounded by moths, she arrived at a polished stone tile and lay down on it, with her legs apart and her face covered by the gauze cloth. She placed the scythe on her breasts and waited. She felt someone lying on her and possessing her to the point of delirium. Then she opened her eyes and, slowly, the light and the darkness became a single thing, a vibrant universe covered by a bluish luminosity that frayed the shadows.

'It's time now,' the woman murmured. 'The harvest moon is rising.'

Bet awoke with a delicious sensation in her body. She gave half a turn on the bed and went back to sleep.

# 9

The morning dawned cloudy, even cool. When she went out onto the balcony, she watered the three flourishing bougainvilleas that formed the colors of the Republican flag, letting out the dampness of the fog. It was early, it couldn't even have been seven o'clock. She didn't mind getting up early. Sunrise was when she felt most alive, and she liked knowing there was a good deal of the day left ahead. She slept the necessary amount of time, four or five hours were quite enough, and she didn't go mad trying to stay in bed after she'd woken up. She wasn't like Happy, able to toss between the sheets until noon.

Luis was a deliveryman for a service of urgent purchases and was almost always traveling. He was rarely able to enjoy the sunrises at the beach. He slept little, considering that while he was asleep he lost time for living. He liked to say he'd sleep when he was dead. Because of that, he took advantage of getting up early whenever he could, watering the bougainvilleas, having a coffee, taking the dog for a walk and playing the piano. He liked music and was a bass player in a rhythm and blues group with some friends from the town. He had a black piano, an upright, in the living-room. He'd bought it from a friend who'd abandoned the building and gone to live with his family in the town.

'There are so many noises here I can't sleep,' he'd said, justifying his move, as if by leaving he'd been a traitor to someone. 'My wife wants to live closer to the children's school.'

'It's a pity, because there are always fewer proprietors and the crisis is doing away with the people who come here for their summer vacations.'

What drew his attention most about the neighbors leaving was the fact they were doing it after the suicide of the woman from 5E. From what people had said, it hadn't been the first suicide in the building. It appeared that in full construction a worker had thrown himself off the roof onto the rocks on the cliff. And what had also happened was the fire on the fourth floor and the death of two children who, frightened by the fire, leapt off the balcony. But all buildings have their stories – there are too many people living in them.

Luis, wary of the morning's dampness and calculating whether it was going to rain or not, was late noticing that the dog was nervously showing him something he was carrying between his teeth. He stooped down for a second to see what it was.

'Damn it! Not again!' he exclaimed angrily, pulling a sparrow from the dog's mouth.

The sparrow was dead, featherless, its neck half chewed. He knew the animal had offered him a hunting trophy, but, instead of stroking him, he threw the bird's body into the garbage bag. He noticed, before closing it, that the bird's belly was swollen and traced in garnet-colored veins, as if the blood were still bubbling inside them. He closed the bag and decided to take the dog out before lunch and, while he was at it, get rid of the little cadaver. He went back to the balcony and finished watering the plants. With the tip of his slipper he cleaned up the feathers that the bird had left on the terrace. He didn't understand why, but in recent months he'd caught half a dozen of them. It wasn't normal for birds (apart from seagulls), to get so close to the balcony, and still less so to fall onto it, as if they'd been paralyzed in the air.

He got dressed, combed his hair with his fingers, and went off to the room to give a kiss to Happy, who was sleeping sideways across the bed. He studied her half-open lips. She looked like a beautiful dwarf dreaming in exquisite worlds. When he saw her like that, with full, pink, and slightly moist lips, he felt an enormous desire to uncover his sex and place the tip of his penis into her mouth. But he'd never done it – he hadn't even spoken to her about his desire. What he did was to scrunch up her hair and, when she woke up, he gave her an affectionate kiss on her forehead and left.

He waited for the elevator. He and Happy lived in apartment E on the fourth floor. The elevator was on the floor above. He pressed the button. He waited with the dog sitting next to his legs until the door opened. He jumped in because he thought there wouldn't be anyone inside. People hadn't lived on the fifth floor for months, or at least as far as he could remember he hadn't seen anyone during the time he and Happy had been there. So he was astonished to find a young woman in a swimsuit with a towel draped off-handedly around her neck.

'I wasn't expecting...'

'I live upstairs,' she chimed in, a little uncomfortably. She stroked the dog's head. 'I'm Nuria, from apartment E on the fifth floor.'

'Luis. I live exactly beneath you.'

'And the dog?'

'What did you say?'

'The dog. What's the dog called?'

'Iggy. It's after...'

'After Iggy Pop?'

'Yes, of course. After him.'

They parted at the entrance. Two by two, she went down the steps to the cliff, and he waited for the dog to pee against one of the garden trees. Later, he also went down to the beach by the same rocky staircase. The dog ran ahead, chasing the bits of branches that Luis threw for him. He picked them up and returned happily, jumping about, just as if he were fetching for him a bird he had just caught. Trophies. The girl from the elevator was already in the water when he sought her with his gaze. He saw her swimming in the direction of some huge rocks that were about five hundred meters away. She seemed to be a good swimmer and he put her out of his mind.

Iggy Pop. Luis hummed 'I Wanna Be Your Dog' by the Stooges. On the beach he picked up a piece of green-painted wood and threw it against the waves. The dog ran after it, submerged himself in the water, and reappeared with a new vitality, as if something had flung him face up from the bottom of the sea. This time he actually squinted at him and they set off running, the pair of them playing at chasing each other, fighting and falling into the damp, gray sand.

It didn't take long before a very gentle, misty rain began to fall.

Happy woke up full of energy after Luis caressed her head and kissed her. She turned over once in the bed and landed mouth downward, her face sunk into the pillow. She wanted to sleep a little longer. *Five minutes more, please*. She spoke out loud as if Luis were still in the room, but heard him closing the door, so she gave another half turn in the bed until she was facing the window. The morning was gray and had cooled down somewhat, but was still warm. She brought her right arm up to her face and smelled it. She kissed it. It didn't sweat, but the skin was tense and hydrated. It smelled of Luis, and Luis smelled soft, but a little bit piquant. Of his first morning coffee with a vestige of black tobacco: that was how Luis smelled. She licked her arm. She gave another turn, freeing her feet from the sheets in which they were wrapped. She opened her eyes and saw the new guitar carefully placed on a wood-and-aluminum base at the end of the clothes cupboard. It was beautiful, with large appliqués in emerald green. Luis had picked it up the day before; they'd made it to order, in the color he'd chosen in a catalog. He was happy when he arrived that night. They went down to have dinner at the restaurant, and there, Berta, the waitress, talked to Happy about their neighbor.

'I could swear she was here last year, but she denies it. In any case, she's easily frightened, very nervous. It may be she heard a woman screaming as she fell from the balcony. She said she went "chop" on the terrace.'

The two women laughed, repeating 'chop, chop. Chop.'

'*Ça va*. And weren't you putting strange things into her head, *darling*?'

'No, girl, the poor thing still doesn't know how the damned seagulls can make such a racket.'

'It's a good thing we still have seagulls left, *is it not*?'

Luis was leaning on the railing looking out onto the beach. He was smoking a tiny bit of marihuana as he spoke with Vidal. He too lived there, alone, and they had a relationship that was almost like a family's, because Vidal was Happy's protector and looked out for her. The entire third floor was his. They knew he was separated from his wife and they had children, but he never had any visitors. They also knew he'd been the building's architect and when he retired, he'd devoted himself to photography. He was always seen with a camera, even at night. In fact, there he was, bending over the railing with Luis, and carrying a camera over his shoulder.

Happy left them talking together and went upstairs by herself. She went to bed early, her ovaries were playing up and she took an anti-inflammatory with a glass of warm milk before she got into bed. Luis had connected the new guitar to the amplifier, put on the headphones, and was trying it out until well into the night.

Still in bed, Happy recreated the previous night step by step. She could remember with precision every minute before she fell asleep. As she did every night, she went over the states of India with their capitals. Sometimes she did it in alphabetical order, others by their position on the map, going from the Bay of Bengal to the Arabian Sea. The previous night she'd slept at the altitude of Kerala, on the *backwaters* surrounded by rice paddies. She and Luis had planned at some point a break in their lives to spend a couple of years getting to know India. But they never managed to find either the money or the time.

With a resigned sigh, she got up and prepared lunch for when Luis came upstairs with Iggy. She would have liked to move the table outside, but it might have rained at any moment. She moved it into the living room. She went out onto the balcony to see if they were on the beach. It had been more than an hour since the dog had been taken for a walk. She looked out at the sea and found it grayish, looking like the old silver of fish scales. She noticed someone swimming, about to arrive at the beach. She waited until the person came out of the water. It was a young woman, with strong legs, her dark hair stuck to her head. She walked over the wet sand

and, bending over, grabbed hold of a towel, also wet. She shook it and spread some sand around her. Then she dried her hair with it and began to go up the open steps in the rock.

'Good grief! *The new neighbor.* She might be easily frightened, but she doesn't appear to be afraid of the sea. *The new neighbor...'*

She entered the house, attracted by the aroma of coffee brewing in the kitchen. She felt delighted and vital, as she did every day.

# 10

Nuria, however, was flagging as she climbed up from the beach. Tired out, she was sweating, despite being soaking wet. It was the first day she had spent swimming such a distance, and without anyone to ask for help if she lost her strength. She was used to swimming. Whenever she could, she would go to the swimming pool and the gymnasium, and didn't exactly consider herself a weak woman. Regardless, the sea imposed a certain respect on her.

When she got out of the water, she stopped to examine the plants on the balcony beneath her apartment. They looked like bougainvilleas, red, yellow, and purple bougainvilleas. They were arranged in such a way as to form the Republican flag. She supposed that apartment was where the young man she'd met in the elevator lived. He was good-looking, she thought. He had a large, burly body, the sort she liked. He wasn't thin: she didn't like thin or small men. She didn't like eels or other slithery creatures either. She smiled when the desire to meet him passed through her head. But it was not to be. Not until she was well. That was possibly a ploy to distract her which, come what may, she should avoid. Because that was where she would lose herself again, decompose herself. She'd loved, surrendered herself, and let herself be guided by the inertia of life as part of a couple. She liked the warmth of that refuge, but it trapped and dissolved her. It was like being caught in a permanent stupor from which she woke up one day and found only pieces of herself. Disconcerted. Dispersed. Defenseless as a baby on a frozen mountain-top.

Not yet. She wasn't going to approach the young man. Perhaps that why she was exhausted: because it cost her so much effort to accept discipline. No one prevented her from going down to the beach and playing with the dog, attracting the young man by playing with him. But no. She went back up to the house and looked out onto the balcony, taking furtive looks to locate him. She found them on the stairs to the cliff, the dog with its tongue hanging out, Luis waving to her with his hand on high. Nuria smiled, but cautiously didn't respond to his greeting, and was glad she'd been prudent when she heard a voice right underneath her, calling for Iggy. She leaned over the railing and found a long blonde mane of hair hanging in the air. She retired indoors, a great deal more saddened than when she'd arrived.

'Iggy, run, run, run!' shouted the long mane in high spirits, hanging from the balcony of apartment E on the fourth floor. 'Iggy, I have meat sausages for you!'

For a moment she thought it was a woman about to explode. Her brain would blow up first, filling the walls with more colors than Induvina's paintings. She grabbed the pendant she was wearing around her neck and remembered she'd forgotten to leave it at home that morning when she'd gone out swimming. Anxious about a loss that hadn't even occurred, she pulled at it forcefully and kissed it. She wanted to call Induvina, and then she wanted to call Bet.

But she stepped into the shower. The warm water on the back of her neck returned her to a state of well-being that kept her immobile, enjoying the tranquility recovered for long enough for the presence of a little happiness to explode in her stomach. She got out of the shower and dried herself off. She missed the mirror. She decided that after lunch she would go into the town and buy the mirror and a sweater, because the nights seemed to be getting cold. And some rubber flip-flops to wear on the beach. She began to feel happy again. She looked over her naked body from a vertical perspective, and saw with satisfaction that she still had a flat belly and pert breasts. She could see her pubic hair in soft little curls like Astrakhan knots. Her thighs without cellulite, her pleasant knees like the smiles of chubby-cheeked children. She herself smiled upon seeing her knees from the level of her eyes... they were really sweet.

The bathroom was a room without windows, with no other possibility of illumination than electric light. She'd been looking over her body illuminated by the light on the ceiling when the lamp blew out and she was left in the dark. A rain of tiny pieces of glass fell on her, and a delicate rainbow advanced over her body and, at last, total darkness reigned. Quiet, wet, smelling clean, she exclaimed:

'Shit, I've left everything all over the place!'

And having said that, angry at herself, she truly believed it was her own fault when the lamp exploded, for having left the bathroom linen, the towel, and the slippers in the middle of the corridor, along with the sand and the algae. She'd planned to clean up afterwards. But yes. It was her fault for not keeping things in order.

As she left the bathroom, a grayish light fell directly onto the wooden floor and left marks, exaggerating the footprints that led from the entrance to the balcony. They were the same footprints she'd seen the day before, but this time they were smaller, those of infant feet or from a very small woman. Tempted to get hold of cleaning products and give them all an extra scrubbing, she followed them. They were so clear and so precise, with that oily substance that suppurated from the wooden boards, she got it into her head to bend over and smell them.

They smelled of a lettuce salad with vinegar and olive oil. She stood up and burst out laughing. She was laughing at herself, at her stupidity in thinking she could see something strange in the footprints. Unexpectedly, a blast of air blew across the living room and continued down the corridor. She heard it beating against the entrance door and walked over to it, convinced she hadn't shut it properly. She was naked, with the towel around her head, and felt cold, a chill that was also unexpected. She jumped as she turned toward the hallway: the woman in the Lycra swimsuit was at the threshold, watching her.

'I was looking for the children.'

'Well they're not here. Damn it! You might have called!'

And the woman left. Nuria's heart was leaping and her head felt so heavy she believed they were going to crack the vertebrae in her neck to smithereens.

She leaned against the wall, panting. A few minutes went by before she felt calm again, and, since she was now indifferent to the stains suppurating from the floor, she repeated like a rosary the soft string of peaceful words her brother Rubén would murmur to her when she was scared and couldn't go to sleep:

'*Until tomorrow, good night, sleep well, goodbye.*'

When she recovered her calm she got dressed and went to the kitchen for a little drink of water. When she turned on the faucet, she noticed a bowl on the table-top blowing smoke. It was half full of tea. She didn't remember making any tea. But she had. There was the bowl. She picked it up to leave it in the sink and, just as she grasped it, she screamed in pain and let it fall to the floor. She'd been scalded. A red, open wound began to appear in the palm of her hand and on her feet, and, peppered by the boiling water, little lumps of lymphatic liquid began to grow. As she worried about the very strange circumstances involving boiling tea, and not even remembering having entered the kitchen that morning, she blamed herself once more.

‘Not again. This is exactly what must not happen. I ought to pay more attention. Much more attention.’

The unexpected appearance of her neighbor and the stupid burn on her foot had put her in a bad mood, and she opted not to go out that day, and to continue looking painstakingly for sounds and scents. Also, the gentle, misty rain of the morning had become a deluge as the hours passed. As the evening drew in, before going down to dinner in the restaurant, she decided that the next day, when she went out to purchase the mirror, she would also buy a radio: there was too much silence in the apartment.

‘A mirror, a sweater, flip-flops and a radio.’ As she repeated the list of things she needed to purchase, she fell asleep that night.

# 11

From where he was, standing up to take his first coffee of the day leaning on the kitchen countertop, he could see a stain on the wall that looked like a cross-eyed skull. The building was full of stains like that, dripping with salt-rot and dampness. It was something that Vidal disliked, because he'd designed a strong, luminous building to stand up to the winds from the sea and the rains that fell, especially from the ferocious southern winds. But its construction was pathetic: it was built in a hurry, with an anxiety to satisfy the urgent demand for spectacular views and the estuary's pleasant summer temperature.

However, this man, familiar with problems, had decided to live there. He'd made this decision because he was lonely. His wife had left with the children years ago, fed up with a strange mania of his: piling things up. All sorts of things. He began by collecting little tin soldiers, but the difficulty lay in his hands, and he ended up compulsively buying any object at all, regardless of its size. The last house he'd shared with his family was near the town. It was pretty, spacious, a chalet from the forties surrounded by poplars, and by a garden of rose-bushes his wife had planted (and he had ruined) by filling it with junk. It had three really large floors that ended up as warehouses, in which it was possible to find anything, from a toy train station to broken-down refrigerators and piles of bags stuffed into boxes and shelves. He also had a horrific collection of nasty old half-rotting clothes, in which awful creatures, such as spiders and rats, made their nests.

When he was engaged to construct the building, his wife and children had already left. He was alone, he felt alone, and that huge pile of things he had accumulated, instead of satisfying him, reminded him exactly of how lonely he was. Whenever he entered the place he felt its coldness, its silence, and the weight of the cold and the silence. His life's weight. So he made the decision to move to the building on the beach. He designed for himself a luminous, diaphanous space, with nothing to disturb him. Like a warehouse. But like a warehouse that would always be empty. He made that decision, and, using the very plans from which he worked, he reserved the front of the third floor, with views of the estuary, with only enough interior walls to preserve the privacy of the bathroom and the bedroom. Even so, while he was designing it, he began to feel sorry for all those things that had piled up for years just to be abandoned, and which were missing him. They would long for his gaze, his presence. They would be so alone, so defenseless.

Then a magnificent idea occurred to him: he would get involved with photography. He bought a camera and for a year during which he constructed the building, he devoted himself to taking photos one by one of all the things that had accompanied him since he was a boy. When he'd finished, he stood in front of the house, looking at it. The thought of buying gasoline and setting fire to it passed through his mind, but he brushed it away. It seemed to him that if he did it, it would be like committing a multiple assassination.

He left the bowl of coffee in the sink and went out to the balcony. The sun hadn't yet come out, but the sky was clear and promised a splendid day. The first bathers, those boys and girls who spent the night drinking in the bars and in the town's discotheques, were already at the beach, talking, swimming, or simply sleeping off a drunken stupor. In the summer months, especially in August, nights in the town were long and intense. There were people in the streets at all hours. Vidal sometimes stayed awake, with his predatory instinct for images totally alert, and would devote himself to going over the terraces to take festive photos. Later, at dawn, he would go to the most depressing places and follow the drugged girls, attracted, just as he used to be by the old things accumulating in his house, by the most miserably obsolete things.

Every day he looked at the photographs that hung on the walls: faces, scenery, houses, objects. That system of accumulation was very much easier and cleaner. It made room for empty space in the apartment: an enormous amount of empty space, so much so that he could even invite an orchestra, place it in the middle of the living room, and a hundred people could listen to it without a problem. The condensation of life was only produced in the shelves stuck to the walls in straight lines and facing the ceiling. Because life weighs tons, he had experience in that. Although it seems that memories don't occupy space, in fact, everything that appears in them has its true weight, as he very well knew.

'That girl,' he said to himself when he saw Nuria coming down the steps to the cliff, towel in hand. 'What's going on in her head?'

Ever since he retired he'd devoted himself to looking around the general area and taking photographs of people in the villages he visited. Especially the boys and girls. He woke up early and walked toward the entrance to the urbanization to await the first bus. He traveled in the bus some twenty-five kilometers, until the last stop. This was in a village beside the River Ulla, and he would get off there, have lunch in a tavern next to the church, and then start the journey back on foot. Sometimes, depending on the weather or the light or his state of mind, or how the milky coffee had tasted, or the little bun of wheat-bread with cheese and ham-hock he'd had for lunch, he would walk back through the mountain villages and make a long stop in a clearing on

Xiabre, where there was a hotel he'd designed himself. A beautiful, cheerful hotel, quite different from the building on the cliff.

That afternoon, coming home from his walk, he saw Nuria sitting in the garden. The girl's skin, white and faded when she'd arrived, had acquired with the days a soft toasted color, and had caught the golden color of the sun. Nuria was leaning slightly on the stone bench, her head tipping backwards, and her face offering itself to the light breeze that made the violet strands of hair in her mane vibrate. She was tranquil. Vidal found her so beautiful in that calm she transmitted he felt an unexpected attraction towards her. He was an old man, but age didn't prevent him from feeling desire, and, fortunately, his sexuality was still there.

Vidal kept on staring at her. She'd changed a lot from that first morning when he'd run into her at breakfast. Her face had distended, she smiled, and her fatigue had completely disappeared. There wasn't a trace of that resentful expression or anguish that marked her eyebrows so deeply. She looked like another woman, even the provocative gaze she directed towards him when she realized he was looking at her and the expression of challenging superiority reminded him of the Nuria he'd photographed about twenty years earlier. He'd never seen again that girl who made love on the beach with her boyfriend, who was almost a kid. Or maybe he had. He'd spent years taking photographs of people, hundreds of faces, many of them repeated dozens of times, but he'd never come across an expression like that happy teenager's.

When he arrived at his apartment he opened a box of photographs. He spread them out over the table and studied them: they were portraits of two girls taken over five years. They looked like each other, yet didn't. They were more different than similar, and, disappointed, he kept them safe by placing them on a shelf. Immediately, he picked up a smaller box on which he'd written 'Quin and Nuria, May 1975,' and opened it. He scattered the contents on top of the table. There were few of them – just five. In some images he saw the building under construction, when Seabeach was little more than a project being announced on the advertising posters and in newspapers. There was a close-up of her, of Nuria. Her huge, lively eyes, the mane profiling her face, and a clean, ingenuous smile flooding the paper.

It was her, he had no doubt of that whatsoever. He would say as much when he saw her again. He was sure she was going to love it when she saw herself so young. Of course. Nuria Uría, the way things turn out, was there.

# 12

Induvina decided he simply couldn't go on like that. He was so sad that he didn't realize he was rummaging every day through Bet's things. In case he found a clue. Something that might reveal to him what had happened and where she was. But finally he realized the obscenity of his behavior and, ashamed of himself, decided he should do away with all her things and get rid of her once and for all. Even if she appeared again, there'd be no more opportunities. The end. Never more Bet and her madness, her caprices, her anger, her talent, her tenderness. Bet's insanity. Out with it. He would get rid of it. The plaster of Paris sculpture of the babies as well. Everything. The mural and the damned photo multiplied on the wall. Away with everything. Period.

In spite of everything, while he searched among Bet's things he opened again the folder with drawings signed by Nuria Uría. Who was that woman? Had she really lived in Lisbon? He thought of one of those artist friends of hers with whom Bet set up performances in the streets. In the folders were geometrical drawings with instructions on measurements and colors. The notes were written in Portuguese. He stopped to look at the heading with the name of the ceramics factory: *Santa Clara de Lisboa*. But no. He still found more things that must have been hers, Nuria's. There was a large envelope that contained a series of wax paintings, seemingly created by a child's hand. They were little houses in colors, and fantastic beings, half witches, half wicked spirits, whose titles were single words written in the same cramped, small, and insecure hand, that accompanied the designs on the tiles: 'Rubén's House,' 'Fairy Godmother,' 'Happy Prince.'

The telephone rang and he crossed the studio from Bet's space to his own, possessed by an excruciating anxiety. In front of the phone, he doubted whether he should pick up or not. He left it up to the answering machine. He stared at it as if he could see the person calling through it. Attention! The digits of a number blinking before his gaze. Then the answering machine jumped and he heard a voice asking for Bet.

'Bet, is that you? Please answer, Bet...' Then he heard the sound of a telephone being hung up.

Induvina's heart beat in his chest. He trembled. He'd wanted her to call so much that it even seemed to be Bet's voice speaking. But no. Bet's voice was without fail grasping and military, and the other woman's sounded delicate and fearful. And nervous. He tried to recover the call, but it was late and he hadn't managed to memorize the telephone number.

He sat down and lit a cigarette. He finished it and smoked another. He poured out a little whisky and drank it slowly, savoring the taste. He remembered he had a visitor that evening. A lady who owned an art gallery, whom he'd met at some inauguration or other, was interested in seeing his paintings and, perhaps, in displaying them. She was going to drop by his studio. *Somebody wanted to see his work.* He stood up, placed his self-esteem on the work table, and cleaned up the remnants of any drugs consumed. Out, everything out! He put on a CD by Wim Mertens on the stereo system and looked at the canvases three meters high that occupied the walls. Immense. The keels of ships painted in tar – that's why the studio stank. Of ships that had just been painted on the coast. The keels of ships ensnared. Immense prows to disrupt the air of the studio. He liked those. One of the ships had rust stains and small colonies of mussels that looked alive. They breathed. Their hermetic shells were as closed as he was. The northern sea was contained inside them, trapped by his hands. He liked his work. He gave the studio a superficial clean and waited for the doorbell to ring. If the gallery owner liked his works, he didn't care about Bet. Bet could stew herself.

He disconnected the telephone so as not to have to worry about calls. He hoped that disconnection would also eliminate the longing for her to call him, but that desire lasted a little bit longer, flying around him like a moth. It never stopped moving while he waited. He looked at his paintings again and again, assuring himself that the best canvases were in full sight, and put on the table the most recent notes. He made coffee. The aroma of fresh coffee reminded him it would be a good idea if he gave himself a bit of a wash. He shaved, and pulled his hair back into a pony-tail. It wouldn't have been a bad idea either to change his clothes, though he didn't have a lot to choose from.

Half an hour later, he was once again standing in front of the paintings. He looked at the clock. The woman was late. He went over to Bet's space and drew the black plastic curtain so the mural wouldn't distract him. He wanted to make a joint, but fought back the drive. He longed for a little more whisky, but he put the bottle away and rinsed the glass in the sink. He took a bowl of bitter coffee and sat down to read a copy of *The European*, which he had rescued from amongst Bet's papers. An article about a perverse sexual confession by an anonymous author attracted his attention, and he decided it fit absolutely with Bet's literary tastes. The borders of the article were filled with little erotic drawings and jellyfish colored in wax. Bored, he closed the magazine at once.

That's when the doorbell rang.

The woman was no longer young, perhaps the same age he was. She was wearing a long, black, almost transparent sleeveless dress, tied at the neck with satin ribbons, also black. Her skin was so white that its contrast with the dress was absolutely stunning. A cloth of cobalt blue kept back her hair from her forehead and let it hang down her back in perfect curls as white as her skin. She wasn't alone: at her side was a young man in a lamentable black and pink tartan shirt, and wearing sunglasses.

'I'm Ana. This is Marco, my son.'

He offered them coffee, but they didn't accept it. Induvina became uncomfortable. It wasn't the first time someone had gone to see his paintings to put together an exhibit. But these were another sort of people, less stiff, perhaps. Less snobbish: that would be the right description. The woman was tough, difficult, didn't pay attention to explanations, and looked at the canvases without showing the slightest emotion. Not even a gleam in her stare: nothing permitted him to deduce whether or not she liked what she was looking at. Furthermore, the young man had disappeared. Suddenly, Induvina had the suspicion that the woman had no interest in what she was looking at nor in what she was listening to, and began to show obvious signs of boredom.

'You have a very personal style,' she observed, but she said it as if she were commenting on everything else that was obvious.

'The style, darling, is constrictive. It's a defect, a limitation.' Induvina wanted to end that idiotic visit as soon as possible.

'What do you think, Marco?' The woman, ignoring Induvina's ironic reply, searched with her gaze for her son.

Marco then came out from behind the plastic curtain. He still had his sunglasses on and was as inexpressive as his mother.

'What do you think?'

'It's very good – impressive,' he said, addressing Induvina. 'How long will it take you to finish the mural? It could be the presiding piece of the gallery. And the sculpture of the dead babies... Do you also do video production? Because it would be...'

Induvina's body turned to sponge. He took a while to recover his voice, and not exactly because of the deception he had just suffered, but because for a very brief moment it passed through his mind to accept Bet's work as his own. It was a moment as brief as a whiplash, but enough to make him feel like an ignoramus. Once he'd begun to recompose himself, he took hold of the woman and the young man by the elbows and, with all the consideration he could muster at that point, accompanied them to the entrance.

He didn't even offer them a word of farewell.

He sat on the sofa and examined his nails, stained by oil paint and tar. He went over to the paintings of the ships and stroked them, as if they were sons hoping to do well. With enormous tenderness – for the art and for himself – he started painting immediately.

All the same, he couldn't avoid thinking of Bet and, for the first time, he was possessed by something similar to hatred.

## 13

After a couple of weeks Nuria felt at ease and a little surprised at not having suffered as much as she'd expected when she stopped taking the medications, which, supposedly, were necessary for her brain to assimilate *reality*. She was sure she had managed it. She considered she was physically and psychologically prepared to accept herself, without fearing this integration would cause within her a cataclysm similar to the tectonic plates of the continent beating against each other. She was prepared to face earthquakes, volcanoes, and erosions, regardless of how aggressive they might be. To assume that life is a continuous process and not a succession of isolated events which, until her retreat to the beach apartment, she had insisted on trying to complete like the pieces of an exhaustingly chaotic and unfinished crossword puzzle. Life: a process. The process: a constant movement, dramatic and inescapable. *Before*, life was always made up of extremes: islands that appeared at low tide, only to disappear submerged in the water to cover the intermediate stages. Without gradations. Living or dying, everything was reduced to that. Perhaps, she thought, a new concept of hers about life that she hadn't even considered a few days before was going to alter her personal perception of time. And of space. Fragmentation would disappear and she would live in a temporal and spatial continuity. And, once that happened, there would be a disappearance of the suspicion of there being many people inhabiting pebbles of time in a kind of parallel set of universes, of which, sadly, they were hardly aware.

She was surprised by the ease with which she had re-educated her body in so little time to actually stop smoking and drinking coffee at all hours. In any case, she stayed alert. She wanted to avoid, as best she could, falling into those apathetic states she knew so well. She was aware that if she did fall into them, she'd have to spend days lying on the bed or the sofa. She couldn't let herself arrive at that situation because she had so little time at her disposal, and she also knew there was nothing she could do. Just wait. Just wait for something, whose nature she never identified, to pull her out of her ennui. And, if that something never happened, she knew the holograms would appear. And, with the holograms, bad humor would arise, discomfort, and, in the end, fury. And, after that, disappearance. *Her* disappearance.

However, she had a couple of days of exhaustion, in which she could hardly do anything but watch television and fall into sick bouts of lethargy, from which she would wake up in a guilty sweat. One particularly hot evening when she was nodding off on the sofa, she awoke with the suspicion that she was not alone. She never felt alone, didn't know what absolute solitude was, but the feeling of company at that hour was so intense she turned her head toward the corridor, expecting to see someone advancing along it. Perhaps it was Bet, who always appeared when she least expected her. It wouldn't be difficult for Bet to find her. Her brother Rubén knew where, and wasn't going to hide it from her. But she didn't see anyone in the corridor: neither Bet nor even the impertinent neighbor in the Lycra swimsuit.

The TV was on. They were showing one of those family dramas that completely absorbed her and prevented her from thinking too hard about her problems. She enjoyed watching those shows until she fell asleep. She turned the TV off in order to pay attention, once again, to the noises in the apartment. Nothing: silence. Only the voices of the bathers that were climbing back, weakened by the relentless beating of the waves. She stood up and ran along the corridor to the kitchen, allowing herself to be guided by a vague impulse, like when she knew she was going to hurt herself and, instead of avoiding the danger, she ran towards it instantly. Because there was something in Nuria that dragged her towards danger, and she felt a persistent love for the shadows that had been with her since she was a little girl. It was as if the dark spaces of her soul drew her irremediably to them.

As she walked she began to feel the house getting colder and that her sweat, suddenly turned into little pins of ice, was sticking into her skin. She was barefoot, dressed only in a pair of cotton shorts and a t-shirt that barely covered her abdomen. Frozen stiff, she gave her body another rubbing with her hands. Her breasts were rigid, her heart beating tenaciously against her. She was sure there was someone in the kitchen, and she longed, before crossing the threshold, that it would be some bird, even a seagull. That there would be *something tangible* in there. There was nothing, merely disorder: a bowl of lettuce leaves, a squeezer with the leftovers of some orange juice she'd made that morning, tea-leaves scattered over the floor, and breadcrumbs. On the table was a glass with some sugar left in it, and a jug of water containing slices of lemon. Eucalyptus branches nodded out onto the railing and, from afar in the blue sky, cut off by the wake of a plane, a dirigible advertised a refreshing cola drink.

More peaceful, comforted by the laborious movement of the airship, she let down her guard. She seemed to hear voices from outside the apartment, in the corridor, but thought they would be children playing. The intense cold vanished and she began to feel hot. She decided to take a shower and go out, to do something to rescue herself from the passivity of the previous days. Take a shower, wash her hair, get dressed, and go for a stroll around the town. Buy fruit and vegetables. Try to talk to someone. Go to the movies, maybe. Have a cold drink on a terrace in front of the pier. She could do a thousand things outside the apartment, but none of them seemed especially attractive to her. It was as if something in there was fighting to hold her back.

In fact, when she was about to get into the shower, she felt an enormous need to sleep, and, putting up no resistance, went back to the living room and to the coziness of the sofa. Just as she was falling asleep, she got hold of the remote control and turned on the television. Voices. Confused voices: a man, children, flustered seagulls. The noises from the beach sounded faded by the distance, but at times they were so clear they seemed to be happening exactly where she was. Disquieted, she found it difficult to breathe under pressure. She felt a wave – invisible but compact – going through the length of the corridor and trapping her. It wasn't her imagination, and neither was she dreaming. It was real: the wave went over and *within* her. She saw perfectly well how the profiles of the furniture had been disfigured, time and the sea having altered their shapes, and how everything around her seemed to turn to liquid. It didn't last very long, she couldn't tell whether it had been a second or an hour. The wave disappeared through the balcony door, attracted by the afternoon sun furiously striking at the sea.

She remained on the sofa, totally immobile, paralyzed by terror. She had the impression something was going through her, that it was entering through her toes, and was moving inside her by dilating her veins, rendering her completely empty and hot, to the point of electrocuting her hair and finally abandoning her. She felt sticky, dirty, coarse. She thought she'd been foolish for suggesting such expectations of herself. Yet again, she doubted herself. She blamed herself and, once the panic had disappeared, she reacted by cleaning up the apartment. Cleaning once again, as if she'd received an order. Cleaning again, as if the disorder of the apartment had anything to do with the filth and coarseness she felt in her entire body.

That night, forcing herself to go out, she went down to the restaurant and made two phone calls. She called her brother; he wasn't at home, but she left him a short message on the answering machine in a cheerful voice, assuring him she was well and inviting him to spend a few days with her at the beach. Then, nervously, she called Induvina. But he didn't answer the phone either and she didn't leave him a message. On hearing Induvina's voice recorded on the answering machine, her innards shrank with tenderness and she grasped the pendant that she wore hanging from her neck.

# 14

The little creature – or perhaps it was Bet – continued to float, as if suspended from a joyful moment.

'Would death be the eternal repetition of a joyful moment?' she asked herself.

Bet remembered the pleasure she felt as a child piercing the packaging that protected the tins of Cola Cao. She would be slow in opening it, tearing it bit by bit with the tip of one of her nails, or driving a pin into it. Would eternally reliving such pleasure be the same as being dead?

Later, the little creature asked herself:

'What would pleasure be? What would living be?'

Digging out a spike piercing one's flesh – that's pleasure.

Bet wanted to wake up.

## 15

Happy was drinking Albariño on the terrace with Vidal. There were lots of people in the restaurant that night, dining outside. The afternoon heat continued, but was attenuated by a soft breeze that wafted an intense smell of sea and gunpowder. Fireworks were being set off on the pier, vibrantly reflected and colorful in the hue of the water. From time to time one heard ecstatic, surprised murmurs on account of the pyrotechnic spectacle. Even Iggy, excited by the explosion of the bombs, seemed exultant and jumped into the air after the stray sparks that died against the cliff.

Nuria, until that time when she went down to make telephone calls, had not been aware of the festive atmosphere in which the town, the beach, and the restaurant had been bubbling all afternoon and evening. Visibly disturbed, she arrived at the restaurant and asked for the phone. She made her call and tried to leave, but the feeling of defeat and the profound desire for despair that possessed her pulled her towards the terrace in search of a catalyst that would cause a sudden outburst of rage and oblige her to surrender and ask for help. She had no idea what the celebration was about, and, at the same time the breeze was beating against her face, she also noticed Iggy's weight, who, clumsy as he was, had thrown himself on top of her, demanding caresses and forcing her into unexpected immobility. After Iggy's assault, and nonplussed by the din of the celebration, she heard a voice calling her. Nuria. Nuria. It was as if the same frozen pins of that afternoon had been stuck into her. Uncomfortably alert, she looked around, and the voice came from the mouth of a young woman standing in front of her, trying to restrain Iggy.

'*You know?* Luis told me you… I'm Happy. *Ça va?*'

Happy was in front of her, agitated, with a silent but cheerful smile. She seized her by an arm and, without asking her, took her off to the table. She asked Berta, the waitress, to bring her a drink, and she served her an Albariño. She introduced her to Vidal, but Nuria avoided extending her hand to him.

'I don't drink alcohol,' said Nuria vehemently.

Nobody seemed to mind that she didn't drink. She ignored the drink. She waited a while, because she wanted to be a pleasant, amiable, attractive woman. With a forced smile she ignored Vidal's questions and tried to pay attention to Happy's muddled conversation, but, at the very moment when an explosion of vibrant creations fell into the estuary, Nuria stood up and departed. Not even Iggy was aware that Nuria had left. She ran silently through the crowd, and disappeared without taking her leave.

Happyleft Vidal at the entrance to the building. She wanted to take Iggy for a walk on the beach so he could pee and she didn't have to wake up too early in the morning. Luis was away: he had to make an urgent trip to deliver merchandise. He wouldn't be back until the middle of the week, and she liked to stay in bed until late, especially when she'd been drinking. During the long stroll on the sand, she couldn't avoid thinking about the neighbor in 5E, and how unsociable she'd seemed. About how ill-tempered she looked that night, how silent she was, how rude she'd been to leave without saying goodbye. In the half month she must have spent there, no one heard any kind of noise from her, let alone footsteps or voices. She had not coincided with her until that night, although she'd seen her swimming in the morning, each time further, each time more prolonged.

She removed her shoes so she could walk more comfortably over the sand. Walking barefoot, the sand felt fresh. She was letting it run between her toes when a wave, gentle and cold, covered her feet and retreated. It tickled her and she smiled. The fireworks had ceased almost half an hour ago, and all that remained on the water was a diffuse fog, like fumes after explosions. There was still a smell of gunpowder and the sea. Iggy was tired and she wanted to sleep, so they turned around and retraced their steps onto the little beach. As they did so to begin their return, Happy raised her eyes to the building. A cold, unreal light left one of the apartments and illuminated the body of a woman on the balcony. She recognized the apartment immediately: it was 5E, the one above hers. It was Nuria's apartment.

The woman on the balcony could only be Nuria, and Nuria was dancing. Or that's what it looked like. She looked as if she were dancing, but she was doing it violently, throwing out her arms, hitting her body, and suddenly standing still for a few moments to hit the air again, as if a brutal rhythm had compelled her to move spasmodically. She stopped and started again. Happy got a fit of the giggles. She didn't stop watching her neighbor's bizarre dance until the trees in the garden prevented her from doing so.

It didn't take long for her to arrive at the building, followed by Iggy, who was walking with his tongue hanging out. The night was still calm – one could only hear the laughter of couples conversing on the restaurant terrace and the music from an orchestra playing on the town pier. Happy took the key out of her pants pocket and introduced it into the keyhole. Then something exploded with a horrific crash: glass panels in the door, which turned into shards and fell in front of her like a horde of furiously boiling bats.

Iggy let out a startled yelp and curled up at Happy's feet, utterly terrified. Happy leaned over him and stroked his head.

'*Ça va, mon petit. Ça va.*'

When she looked at the portal again, expecting to find her neighbor, she didn't see a thing. There was nobody around. The dolphins were floating on the white marble, illuminated by the fading light of the streetlamps. Then she noticed the darkness of the staircase, warning her to wait for a period of time before she entered.

# 16

Nuria discovered the shattering of the portal's glass panels the following day, when she went out to take her long morning swim. She woke up tired, although she'd gone to bed early. Yesterday afternoon had been strange, with that delirium in which she'd felt traversed by a kind of widening wave. That night she'd slept a lot, sweetened by a pleasant dream of which she still remembered a tiny fragment upon awakening. She recalled something like an embrace, a delightful dissolution of the embrace someone was giving her, but she didn't know who. Perhaps it was more a desire than a real dream. Perhaps.

When she saw the broken glass she stepped around it at a distance, as if she'd never been there. She only knew her feet hadn't been pierced by flying glass. She'd seen Iggy on the beach chasing seagulls. Happy was walking some fifty meters behind the dog, dressed in denim pants cut off at thigh-level and a long-sleeved woolen sweater. She wore Wellingtons and her blonde hair drawn back.

Nuria tried to avoid meeting anyone, pretending to be in a hurry to get into the water. She still hadn't composed herself the way she'd wanted, still not managed to present the image of the pleasant, cheerful and coherent woman she'd sought to appear. Even so, regardless of the speed at which she walked to the sea, Iggy intercepted her and, behind him, Happy appeared.

'*Morning, darling,*' she greeted her.

Nuria had noticed the previous night the distinctive form of speech of that curious young woman, mixing voices and languages. She would suddenly put on the voice of a little girl, and then she'd speak like a man. She switched from French to English and to Galician, as if it were the most natural thing in the world. Nuria wondered what had happened to her real voice, and in what circumstances she'd use it. And it didn't take long for her to find out, because – suddenly making herself sound serious in a low but masterful tone – Happy spoke to her of the night before.

'I saw you last night, you were dancing like a lunatic. Then I saw you at the portal. Is there something wrong with your head, or what?'

'What are you saying?'

'You were indoors – it was you. You were whacking the glass.'

'I wasn't...' but she doubted it.

It couldn't have been, she was in bed. She'd left Vidal and Happy and escaped without a sound. That's what happened. It was true she'd been rude. She hadn't said goodbye or even thanked them for inviting her to a glass of wine. But that was all. Then she'd gone up to her apartment and gone to bed. She fell asleep in no time – that's all she could remember: that she'd gotten into bed and hadn't even put on the radio. She'd suddenly fallen asleep, not having turned over in bed once. She'd woken up tired, but that was normal. She almost always awoke exhausted, as if an enormous event had taken place when she dreamed.

It had happened so often that people told her she did things she didn't remember that she doubted. She became nervous, and the blood rose to her head, throbbing at her temples. Happy must be mistaken, Nuria couldn't understand her insistence. She tried to control her sudden anger by breathing slowly, concentrating on the girl's lips, which became humid as she spoke. One of those hurtful, unexpected memories passed through her head and put a gesture of pain on her face.

Once, a long time ago, during one of her family's habitual housing moves owing to her father's work, she'd met a girl the same age as she was. They'd met on the patio of the building they'd moved into. She, Nuria, was building a little toy house of blocks that piled up in a corner of the patio, and the other girl appeared and started staring at her. Neither of them said a word. Suddenly, Nuria developed an irrational hatred towards that girl who was silently staring at her and threw a fragment of a block of concrete at her. A wound opened in her head that bubbled up a great deal of blood. But because the girl kept silent, without a complaint, without crying, surprised by the blow, Nuria wanted to hit her, insult her, kick her. And she hit her and insulted her and, as she lay on the floor, she kicked her, and Nuria felt a sweet pleasure, like when she had dug out with a needle a splinter that had got stuck in her foot, or had popped a pimple. The more she burrowed into the pimple, the more pleasure and fury she felt. The pleasure and fury were so great that she would have left the little girl in tiny pieces if she herself had not suddenly fallen to the floor in a faint. Nuria never learned exactly what had happened, although she remembered herself enveloped in a yellow light she would forever associate with anger.

And that same anger was to appear as long as Happy accused her of madness, so tranquil and so beautiful, so marvelously shocked and, at the same time, so confident in herself. It wasn't easy for her to control that paroxysm, but, in the midst of the fog clouding her head, an affectionate voice guided her to the morning sun:

'*Ça va? Ça va,* darling?'

The fragrance of toast and coffee being prepared in the restaurant for lunch definitively caused her to regain her composure and recover her desire to be cheerful and amiable. She would have to swim, become extenuated, feel painfully exhausted in order to recuperate her equilibrium and be able to suppress that violent outburst. She noticed a shell that was shining at her left foot and was obviously very old – as worn out as she was. Tiredness possessed her as if she'd been walking for centuries, without a destiny to welcome her, without allowing herself to remove her shoes and rest, open her hands and be thankful: 'My God, at last I'm at peace, at last I'm alone!'

'I'm fine, nothing's the matter.'

Nuria felt nauseous and found a place within the scenography surrounding her: the water at the beach in the morning, the dog that whimpered, the girl that watched her and the seagulls that left footprints in the sand.

'Forgive me, *darling*,' Happy said almost into her ear, recovering again that fictitious tone of voice, this time moving her eyes from side to side, like a bad girl being repentant. 'I had too much to drink yesterday, *sorry*. *Okay?* I must have seen shadows in the portal. *You know?* I drank a lot yesterday, Luis isn't here. I invite you to a coffee, later, whenever you like.'

Before she went underwater, Nuria decided, challengingly, to accept Happy's invitation, and, with a complacent gesture, turned to face her.

'If you like, we can have coffee after lunch. At four?'

'*Okay*. At four.'

After Nuria had swum completely submerged for a couple of minutes, she opened her mouth to breathe when her head reached the surface. An odd satisfaction possessed her, something like the certainty that nobody could ever detain her. No one, ever, would be able to dominate her. She was a fish, she was an alga, a sea-horse. She was strong, she was large, she was immense. She shone in the light of the morning.

She heard the motorboats making trails on the estuary and noticed the warmth of the sun's rays on the back of her neck. She turned her head to see Happy on the beach. She saw her, smiled with satisfaction, and dived underwater again. But not much time had passed before the sea turned yellow around them. She doubted, panted, and came up to the surface again. She breathed as if she were on the edge of death. Everything was yellow everywhere. That light again, the light of the wheat fields burned by the summer drought, of the fruit rotting under the impenitent sun. That light which illuminated men and women at sunset, when they opened their mouths a little and showed their dry tongues and their thirsty palates. That sick light she'd escaped from was there: the yellow light of dead peaches.

And she swam with all her strength, against herself.

# 17

Stunned by the heat, Induvina lay down on the sofa. He was reading one of Bet's books, where an account of the lives of women saints and the martyrdom to which they'd been subjected were written in great detail, as well as the immolations, privations, and humiliations of each one. Bet was particularly attracted to psychopathy. But to the hedonist Induvina, those aberrations, described with such specificity in the book, didn't interest him at all. He was no longer able to concentrate on the reading and began to take on a light sleepiness. With the sluggishness, the air seemed more toxic than usual in his studio.

He was nodding off when he realized that someone was looking at him. Startled, he opened his eyes, and saw the amicable face of a woman bending over him. It was

Violeta, a friend with whom he'd maintained intermittent amorous relationships, but whom he'd always thought highly of and considered a person close to him, someone he could confide in. They'd become distanced in the course of the last two years during his relationship with Bet, more than anything because she didn't like to see him so subjected – 'exactly that, *subjected*' was how she told him she saw it – and it bored her enormously that he never spoke of anything but that girl, what he'd learned from that girl, how creative and intelligent that girl was.

'Don't you ever close the door?' she asked him, pushing him so he'd get up.

'What for? Who's going to steal a painting three meters high?' They kissed and embraced. Induvina put his chin on her shoulder and rubbed her back. Then, looking into her eyes, he asked her what she was doing there.

'Somebody told me you were stupidly sad and lonely. Shall I make some coffee?'

Induvina cleared the table while she turned on the electric coffee-maker.

'At least you're working.'

He smiled, contented. In the past few days he'd painted without rest, and it hadn't mattered whether he slept or not. He liked what he was doing. There were moments when he noticed he abandoned his body and climbed up to the roof and saw himself painting down below. Violeta searched among the CDs, selected *Songs for Drella* by Lou Reed and John Cale, and put it on his stereo system. Before sitting down at the table, she made some approving comment about Induvina's musical tastes. He went ahead and served the coffee so that each had a thick, opaque glass. For a while they didn't say anything, and merely looked at each other as they pressed each other's hands, which they'd placed on the table.

'We seem to feel, whenever we get profound, that everything around us gets profound with us, and it's not like that. You're sad, but it's a luminous day out there, the buildings are still standing, and many people are laughing happily.'

'The best thing would be to put an end to this as soon as possible,' he said, moving his gaze to the lantern.

'It was like an earthquake,' she said with precision. 'Too destabilizing for you.'

'I've never had sex as glorious and at the same time as sad,' said Induvina wearily. He rubbed his eyes.

'Well, whenever I lose a lover, I believe it's a thing nobody would ever get over. But a better lover, or a different one, always appears.'

'Maybe. But now all her things are there,' he said, pointing without looking at Bet's part of the studio. 'I can't stop obsessing about her never having existed – that in reality I dreamed of her.'

'Get rid of them,' advised Violeta with apparent light-heartedness, trying to hide the desire that Induvina should definitively free himself from Bet.

'I can't. Not because of me, but because she didn't bring any clothes or books. And I can't throw anything out. I still believe she might suddenly appear, like she's done before.'

'That's crazy! It's been three weeks since she left,' his friend answered brusquely. 'Do you really think she's going to come back?'

‘Yes. She might. I don’t know. She said not, but I’m not sure.’

‘Why don’t you call her brother? Let him make the decision, without getting you mixed up in it.’

Induvina doubted whether to phone Bet’s brother Rubén, but in the end it didn’t seem like a good idea. Calling him would be humiliating, especially bearing in mind it was Bet who’d decided to leave. Also, he didn’t like that guy too much. Though he’d only seen him a couple of times, they didn’t get on at all. He had a possessive, despotic manner of treating Bet, blackmailing her with threats Induvina didn’t understand, and getting her to treat the entire world with contempt.

He remembered a dinner at the studio. It was during the first months of their relationship. Bet was resplendent, exultant. Induvina, enamored, had turned himself into the most generous and communicative man in the world: nobody, not even Violeta, had ever seen him like that, and perhaps owing to this – the way he’d be dazzling for Bet and never for her – she had begun to distance herself from him in those early days.

Bet was determined to organize that dinner: they’d invite their closest friends, it would be fun. Those were the days just before Christmas – they ordered omelets and hors d’oeuvres from a restaurant in their neighborhood and brought in all kinds of drinks. Induvina had his provisions of cocaine, and Rubén appeared with the odd extra gram. It was too cold, they lit the big coal-fired stove and got together around it. There must have been a dozen people. Bet invited only her brother, saying that her friends didn't live in the city. Induvina managed to rally some friends, and Violeta and her companion were also there during those months. Things didn't seem to be warming up a great deal, so Rubén proposed a game.

'I'm sure all of us, if we could, would kill someone.'

Some people looked at him as if they didn't trust him, but, in general, everybody paid attention.

'Okay, but as we're not going to kill anyone, I propose that at least we should say who we'd like to have die. And Daddy and Mommy don't count.'

A shocked, awkward, icy silence descended. And suddenly Violeta burst out in a guffaw.

'What a good idea! This is like doing mass therapy. I'll start!'

Induvina couldn't believe it. One by one, uninhibited by drinks and the drug, they began sentencing people they knew to death. There were some compassionate individuals who wanted a particular person to die, as well as all the persons who loved them, so they wouldn't suffer that person's loss. Bet desired the death of a woman friend whom only her brother knew, a friend who seemed to have spent her entire life giving her a hard time.

Rubén was delighted. Proud of having let loose such a bunch of psychopaths, he was smiling cruelly and greedily.

When it was his turn, Induvina refused to sentence anybody. Livid, he said they were all crazy and he wanted them to leave.

'You're all sick.'

'And you're a hypocrite,' answered Rubén, irritated.

And there the game ended. The people who'd laughed with evident obscenity (not counting Rubén and Bet) lost their impetus, and, in the silence before leaving the studio, turned out to be ashamed, naked, and puritanical for allowing themselves to be manipulated.

Bet didn't see Rubén again until months later, when he accompanied her to the studio after she'd disappeared for several days. They both sat down to talk, exclusively, confidently, she displaying in front of him a droll indifference. How he'd hated them! Lying in bed (because they'd been there until dawn), he heard how they laughed, how they talked, intoxicated with life, availing themselves of cocaine, alcohol, and insolence.

'Call Rubén. He'll know what to do,' Violeta insisted.

Making the decision was tough for him. But he was convinced by his friend's observations regarding the need to do away immediately with that agony. The truth was that, after the party in the studio, Violeta hated Rubén and Bet profoundly. And over time, that hatred turned into a sweet compulsion that awaited the moment of revenge. She never forgave them for being the first to fall into the trap, for exhibiting in public desires never before confessed, even to herself.

So Induvina phoned Rubén, in Violet's presence. The conversation was cordial: Bet's brother was understanding, and even told Induvina he wanted to talk to him, calmly. He invited him to lunch the following day, but, aware that having lunch together would imply too much time in the company of the young man, Induvina said no.

'I'd prefer you to come over and decide what to do with her things.'

But Rubén must have said something to make Induvina, unexpectedly, agree to meet him the following Sunday morning. Violeta, who was listening for the outcome of the conversation, raised her arms and let them fall in a gesture of desperation.

'It doesn't matter, don't worry about it,' answered Induvina, facing up to what she meant. 'There's something going on – I don't know, but there's something that isn't right.'

## 18

'I see holograms' was how she explained it to Happy.

'Holograms, *darling*?' Happy didn't have the slightest idea what *see holograms* meant.

'Yes, like projections, as if I could pass through the things I see, regardless of how solid they are.'

'But that must be extremely bothersome, *is it not*?'

'No. I'm used to it. The problem is it gives me a sensation of provisionality, as if what I'm living through isn't real. I don't know – it's as if I were dreaming all the time, as if I hadn't been born yet.'

Nuria wasn't aware, but that permanent provisionality she'd talked about was converting her into an irresponsible and disorganized being. There were infantile attitudes in her, as if she were a little girl in a waiting room, awaiting the time to be alive. Life still wasn't *that*. Real life would come later, at some point. *Later*. Someday she'd wake up and she'd be *within* a time when the law of gravity would acquire all its meaning, and stones would fall, and women who flung themselves from a fifth floor would be splattered over the dolphins on the terrace. That was logic. She would also hear voices calling for her and, when she answered the call, she'd find someone waiting for her. They wouldn't be sterile words pronounced aloud uselessly, coming from nowhere, from nobody. There'd be a mouth, there'd be lips, there'd be eyes, hands... there'd be some intention behind the invocation.

The voices, amid the holograms, could proceed from anywhere. In spherical time they could come at any moment. At that joyful moment when she was a mother lying on a grass bed with primitive light, for example. Or also when she was a small being floating inside a nutshell. But that was something she really couldn't say to Happy. She wouldn't understand it, she would come to the same conclusion as the rest of the world: Nuria is sick in the head. And Nuria doesn't want anyone to think that of her. Nuria is there, a recluse in that horrifying building, to show the world she's a complete, strong person, and coherent. And above all, cheerful and brilliant. She wants to shine brilliantly among people. She wants to be incomparable and resplendent like the harvest moon.

But she didn't tell Happy she remembers things, although at times it wasn't very clear to her if they *really* happened. She remembers, for example, a conversation with Induvina, once when Bet wasn't there. She told him that one day, as a child, she experienced a kind of revelation: she was staring at herself in the mirror. Staring at herself in the mirror was something she did frequently, until she got to the point where her eyes would join in a horizontal line, a single eye lengthened from one ear to the other. Given over to that process of the deformation of her own face, the idea came to mind that there was no such thing as a soul. What did exist was the brain: the brain was *really* the soul. Induvina said she was right, and told her she was possibly exercising, unbeknownst to herself, a kind of meditation that led her to that conclusion. He talked to her about neurotransmitters and drugs.

'Because God, in reality, is inside a neuron, or perhaps he's a gene,' the painter said sententiously.

That night they consumed Colombian hashish that Induvina cultivated in huge pots beneath the lantern in the studio. They smoked the dried flowers mixed with blonde tobacco and mint. As they smoked, the mint opened up their lungs and Nuria breathed it in with pleasure, with a deceptive sensation of health and freshness. Induvina explained to her that hashish put a brake on time, that it made the brain go back in time to the first animals, when the human being was a hunter, and time passed for the hunter as if he were watching stills from a film.

'Like when you're about to die. D'you know what I'm saying? Like when you have a car accident and your life passes through your head. That's the work of hashish.'

'Well, I see holograms,' she confessed to him.

'Holograms?'

'Yes, like projections. And I hear voices that... but you're going to believe I'm crazy.'

'Do you know what would happen,' interrupted Induvina, 'if we could hear what people are thinking? We'd hear really twisted hogwash, craziness. We're all psychopaths, at least in thought.'

That was why she liked Induvina: he didn't judge her. Although she knew he didn't like talking with her at all. If he was drunk, yes, for sure he'd tolerate her and would converse on the interesting things she'd talk to Bet about. He would lose his inhibition, become especially amiable, and they'd talk peacefully, although he would always end up talking about Bet's issues. Sometimes, Nuria even doubted whether Induvina realized she was there, whether he knew her, because he didn't seem to show the least interest in her. She had the impression he completely ignored her, and only consented to her being near him for Bet's sake. And, when she was certain this had happened, Nuria clung to the pendant she wore around her neck and kissed it.

'Who's Bet?' inquired Happy with interest.

'A friend.'

'What a strange name. You know? It sounds like *bête*, "beast" in French.'

Nuria put on a made-up expression of innocence. There was something about Happy she found attractive, dangerously attractive. Perhaps it was that trace of vulnerability that appeared when she separated her fleshy lips to speak. Or perhaps it was the way she made a downward arch to the corners of her mouth. When she stopped smiling, her lips met and the corners fell slightly, in a sad gesture of defeat. In her disposition to victimization, she intuited the possibility of manipulation. The acceptance of humiliation. And that made Nuria feel strong, even blatantly dominating. It wouldn't be difficult to experience with Happy the new appearance she herself was acquiring, of a jovial, kind, coherent, and reunified woman.

Since the beginning of their conversation, confessions were exchanged until Happy's entire confidence was won over. Because of that she spoke to her about holograms, and because of that she talked to her about Induvina and mentioned Bet. Although the part about Bet was not done purposely. She didn't want to take her to the beach, she didn't even want to invoke her by naming her. Happy, on the other hand, confessed her problems with food, the totally dependent relationship she maintained with Luis, who treated her as if she were a little girl.

'And why do you talk like that? I mean, why do you mix up languages and change your voice?'

'*Ça va, ça va,*' she responded. 'My father is an Englishman, my mother Belgian. I lived in many countries. By the way, you must come with me to a place you're going to like, and that way you're also going to leave this hole.'

Time passed peacefully until Luis arrived. Nuria and Happy saw each other every day. They took Iggy for walks, got shopping done, went to the movies. They sunbathed nude in a mist at some distance from the urbanization. But Nuria at no point abandoned her daily discipline: swimming, walking, overdoing her exercises. She never again felt the tendency to discontinue following the routine that had possessed her the week before, and she was active at all hours. Neither did she see the neighbor with the swimsuit again, nor did she have to worry about the stains in the form of footprints going up and down the corridor. It was as if they'd disappeared, perhaps because in the end she'd managed to eliminate them with so much scrubbing.

Furthermore, she felt well. She was fun-loving and lucid, seeing herself as ingenious and engaging. She chatted with everyone, let herself be treated with affection by the children of the urbanization, who would see her arrive sweating after the long walks in the afternoon. She enjoyed life to the full: the scent of eucalyptus and the sea, the scintillating coloring of the kites that the children flew on the beach; she enjoyed the music that wafted up from Happy's apartment and encouraged her to eat from time to time something apart from salad and fruit. She even ventured, prudently, to have some fresh wine during the early hours of the night, savoring it and allowing the acidity to awaken her palate. She could feel without her senses becoming storms, she could enjoy every emotion, because suddenly her brain was capable of directing all of them without becoming obstructed.

'I believe that what's happening to me,' she confessed to Induvina, 'is that my head doesn't process well all the information it receives. It gets jammed up, blocked, and goes mad.'

'Everything your brain does is because it just needs to,' he responded. 'Let it go ahead and do that: allow it to. You'll feel better.'

# 19

*'Come on, darling,'* Happy urged her.

Happy and Iggy were on the beach when Nuria emerged from the sea. She was panting and doubled up over her knees, pressing them so she wouldn't lose her balance. As she got up, she saw the blue building standing high above Happy's head, as dirty and ugly as a threat. Her heart was beating so fast she feared she would have a heart attack. She swam for an hour to the limit of her strength, swallowing so much water she felt as if there was a ball of salt in her stomach and her ears were blocked.

Happy spread out the towel Nuria always left on the sand to cover up the little bag where she kept her keys and her pendant. Before accepting the towel Happy was offering, Nuria took out the pendant and placed it around her neck. She kissed it with discreet devotion, as if it were a crucifix. Iggy licked the salt off her legs, and Happy looked at her with total admiration, attentive to anything she might need.

*'Ça va?'*

No. Nuria wasn't well. She collapsed onto the sand, making an effort to control the rhythm of her breathing. She put her head on the towel and let herself be carried away by the Donald Duck song that Happy had started to sing, imitating the voice of the Disney character. *The new neighbor... Oh, Pete, Pete*. She burst out laughing in an uncontrollable guffaw.

Happy wanted to take Nuria to the place she'd told her about a few days back, to the place she'd said she would like. They had lunch on the restaurant terrace and, when the first bathers spread their towels out on the sand and stuck their parasols into it, they came out facing the mountain. They walked for a couple of hours along dirt paths, among prickly bushes and rocks, always climbing. Nuria wasn't wearing the right sort of footwear for a walk like that, on slippery moss and stones that hurt the soles of her feet. She was wearing those canvas slippers she'd bought the afternoon she arrived in town.

'D'you know? I had some gorgeous sandals I left in a shoe store,' she commented to Happy without discontinuing the walk. 'They're bound to be pretty on you.'

But Happy cannot have heard her. She was walking ahead of her, with more effort than Nuria. Every now and then she stopped and asked her to look back, as the views of the estuary became ever more impressive. Much more so than the view from her apartment. The landscape trembled among the trees under the extreme midday light. Nuria, despite all her progress, still sometimes saw the countryside as a scenography, but precisely because of that she found within it a suggestive solemnity. The flat colors, especially the blues and greens, contrasted with the brilliant rooftops of a nearby village. Smoke was puffing out of its chimneys, smelling of a mixture of mallow flowers and grass mowed and eaten. They'd abandoned the path to cross a meadow of waving rye, surrounded by birches. Happy suggested sitting in the shade, and took out of her backpack an orange and a bottle of water for each of them.

'Is there a long way to go?' Nuria asked.

'No, we're almost there.'

Happy then showed her some small houses in cinnamon and salmon rose colors that stood out, at their tallest, among the trunks of the birches. They were tiny little houses which, at that point in the summer, were almost confused with the color of the rocks and the low-lying dry bushes and trees.

'*It's my hostel,*' said Happy with pride.

'Do you live there?'

'No, *darling*. It's mine.'

Surprised, Nuria looked at her. Happy was peeling her orange very slowly and carefully: its skin let out a bright, acidic liquid, which settled on her nails. She noticed Happy's nails were bitten down to the skin, with white spots. She'd never noticed them before, perhaps because previously she'd only noticed her mouth, its corners, and her diluted green eyes that were almost transparent. Also, when she saw Happy sitting down with her knees making visible marks under her olive-green pants, she realized how thin she was.

Happy barely sucked on a couple of segments and threw the rest of the orange at the trees. At that moment she seemed like an aggravated, abhorred child. Even so, to Nuria she'd become more interesting: she owned a hotel.

In Nuria's head a series of thoughts not new to her were forming a chain: she would make herself an intimate friend of Happy's and, if one day something awful happened to her, like dying in an accident, the hotel would be hers. And why not Luis's? Curiously, she was not ashamed of these kinds of thoughts, they didn't hurt her like the others that came to her unexpectedly. And they didn't hurt her because those thoughts were hers, she recognized them as hers, and she didn't know where the others – the painful ones – emerged from.

During the final walk to the group of houses that Happy called *my hostel*, Nuria discovered that Happy's parents were leaving children and little hotels all over the world. It seemed to her an extraordinary way of life. Perhaps, when Happy died and she became the owner of the hotel (and also of Luis), she too could live like that, from voyage to voyage. She'd go to California, to Thailand, to Argentina. That's where Happy's brothers and sisters were. Her parents were established in Nairobi at that point.

In a sudden revolt, Iggy began to run, and Happy smiled, satisfied.

'We're almost there. *You know?* We've arrived.'

In a fenced-off area of myrtles, a plank crowned with the word 'Xiabre' in iron letters opened onto a patio covered with broken shells and shining pebbles. Bushes of marguerites and hydrangeas in bloom formed an ample circle around the patio, faced by the doors and windows of a dozen tiled houses in the form of a terrace. There were large cacti, surprising in that place. The colors of the houses, the cacti, and the intense light reflected by the shells and the pebbles caused an impression of being out of place, of belonging to warmer and drier climes. A colony of bi-colored cats, some with traces of Siamese origin, looked splendid in the sunshine. Iggy scared them off by barking at them.

'*Ça va?*' asked Happy, seeing the enthusiasm in Nuria's eyes.

'*Ça va,*' answered Nuria, incredulously.

'Vidal designed the houses and the site. It's lovely, isn't it?'

'The photographer?'

'*Ja*. But in fact he's an architect. He's like a godfather to me, he's a friend of my parents.'

Beyond the patio was a grill at which a man wearing a bathing suit was roasting vegetables and a chicken cut into pieces. Under an arbor of wisteria, two more men and a woman were drinking beer. Happy greeted them and conversed with them in German for a few minutes. She didn't seem very comfortable speaking that language and switched intermittently into English and French. One of the men greeted Nuria in Spanish, inviting her to a beer. During the previous days with Happy, she'd had a little wine. Since then, she'd made no objections to drinking beer.

They had lunch there, in the shade of the wisteria. When the meal itself was actually over, the conversation extended beyond what was expected, and it was already time to return to the beach when two young men carrying knapsacks appeared. Happy put them up in one of the houses, spent some time with them and, when she returned, asked Nuria if she felt like staying there that night.

'I don't know, I don't believe so.'

She searched for convincing excuses to get back. She didn't have any real reason to do so, but it was as if it anguished her to spend so much time away, far from her nest. She wasn't trying to keep up with the routine she'd imposed upon herself and which had cost her so much effort, but with something not even she could understand: there, in the middle of the countryside, she felt the apartment calling to her. With a sad gesture, she confessed to Happy that she ought to go swimming the next day. If she didn't swim, she wouldn't feel well.

'There are people that sublimate physical exercise,' a man's rounded, hard, but cracked voice, which seemed to spring from a fissure in his lungs, interrupted her excuses.

Nuria turned around and discovered old Vidal. She hadn't recognized his voice. The other times he'd spoken with her, he'd done so timidly, with less authority. She hadn't seen him arrive, either, but, despite everything, it appeared he'd been sitting on the wicker chair half the afternoon. She didn't know why this man made her feel such dislike. She suspected that she knew him or, even worse, that he was spying on her. For a moment, in one of those sudden images, she placed him in an old dream. But it didn't seem possible for her to dream of people she didn't know; how was she going to dream of someone she'd never seen in her whole life?

'There are people who try to extenuate themselves by swimming in order to conceal other problems,' Vidal insisted. 'You may well be one of those people.'

'And you are an insolent person!' she responded with irritation.

'I might be, but, above all, I'm an observer. I've been observing people for many years now. It's a good excuse that keeps me apart from humanity, which, all else being equal, doesn't interest me in the least. And I observe you and know you.'

But, to Nuria, those words sounded distant, like an echo, and she didn't bother to answer. She'd had too much beer and felt sluggish. She couldn't think clearly, and couldn't be brilliant or ingenious, so she preferred to keep silent. She noticed the presence of more people there, and saw a motorbike covered in dust within the area fenced off by planks.

She lost sight of Happy, who didn't take long in appearing with a woman whom Nuria hadn't seen before. The two of them appeared with their arms linked, laughing. The woman was a little shorter than Happy, had a little boy's haircut, and was dressed in motorcycle leathers: black ones, printed with red rays that climbed up her legs. She was wearing aviator sunglasses with green shades, which, when removed, revealed a pair of shining eyes, outlined in kohl. Her face was burnt, and its red color, together with the black outline, accentuated the light in her eyes. They sparkled as though they were also blazing inside.

'Nuria, this is Federica.'

They greeted each other by shaking hands.

After that she couldn't keep her eyes off Federica, whom she'd disliked the minute she saw her. She seemed too peevish and noisy, one of those people who love being the center of attention. She reminded her of Bet. Perhaps because of that she'd sensed the instantaneous rejection. All the same, she didn't feel able to keep her eyes off her when she sat at the table and greeted people as if she were someone important. Behind her, there appeared another woman with a motorcycle helmet in her hands. She was robust, tough, and displayed a tattoo of spines that covered her right forearm.

'*Hey, darling,*' said Happy, as she laid her hand on Nuria's shoulder. 'Antón has a car for the drive down. I'm staying on.'

Antón was one of caretakers at the hotel, in charge of repairs and keeping the garden in order. And keeping the pantry supplied. He was a man of about forty who seemed accustomed to getting on with all those foreign people. Old Vidal, after taking some photos of the tattooed spines, decided to go down with him.

'And you, girl, aren't you coming?' he asked Nuria.

'No. No.'

Perhaps if the question hadn't been asked by Vidal, she would have made another decision. Perhaps, because that woman who reminded her of Bet, who inhibited her to the point of preventing her from speaking and forcing her to step back to a secondary plane, exercised over her an irremediable attraction: the inexplicable attraction of things people find repugnant, like the smell of excrement or putrefaction. Despite that, sometimes when she remained silent and was curled up in a chair, she seemed gentle and calm. Also, in those moments she, too, reminded her of someone. She was like many people rolled into one, and they all seemed familiar to Nuria.

The hours began to disintegrate in the din of chaotic and multilingual conversations. Nuria, insistently silent, was going from English to French, from German to Galician, interpreting the conversations based on the words she understood.

'I once tried a curious remedy,' Federica intervened. 'Are you familiar with electric fish?'

The interest of some people centered on the woman, and even Nuria felt obliged to listen to her. Federica had a great ability to attract attention, and also her way of interfering in conversations reminded her of Bet.

'I hurt my foot once, walking through a place on the Adriatic coast. It got swollen and was terribly painful. There weren't any doctors nearby, but after a few hours a fisherman appeared with a pair of live fish. First he put one on me: it gave off some impressive electric discharges. When that fish died, he put the second one on me until my foot went numb and was cured. It never hurt me again.'

Somebody else had heard tell of those electric fishes and made the point that, in antiquity, the Greeks used them to cure madness, as a primitive antecedent of electric shock. Later, Federica, emboldened by the bottle of Albariño she'd consumed almost all by herself, continued to interrupt conversations with her personal anecdotes, which predisposed Nuria against her even more. Bet was exactly the same: she couldn't talk about anything apart from herself, and also her eyes got smaller when she'd had too much to drink. And on her underlined eyes, like on that other woman's, black insects that never stopped moving were dashing around. She decided to withdraw, mystified by the beer and the chaotic conversations.

The night looked perfect. The sky and the distant sea were clear and beautiful, and looked clean in the light of the moon. Lying in bed, Nuria thought constantly about the electric fish and their beneficial effects. She thought bad things can cure, pain can cure, an electric discharge calms pain. Bet is bad, she can be cured, such an idea had never occurred to her. *Until tomorrow, good night, sleep well, goodbye.* And Nuria fell asleep. But she slept disturbed by a dream in which she occupied a bed under an oak tree. She was lying in a perfectly made bed, situated beneath an oak and at the side of a road on which old Vidal had arrived on foot, his camera on his shoulder. There were fishes there, too. In reality the camera was a horrific, voracious fish with an enormous, tubular tongue that tried to penetrate her.

In the morning, Happy took a long time waking up. She'd gone to bed late, almost at dawn. As Nuria had lunch, she waited for her at the tables arranged on the patio. She was nervous, missing the hours of swimming with which she started the day, but became calm with the idea of walking down to the village. Two hours of intense walking would be enough. Some people were early risers and had left already. The women on the motorbike coincided with Nuria. Federica was radiant: her hair was short, almost white, worn in a mess on her head, as if she'd just washed it and didn't comb it. Her complexion, reddened by the night, was at this point golden and smooth, and her eyes, already profiled in kohl, directed a disapproving stare at her. Or that was how Nuria interpreted it, because, in fact, the gaze of that woman was resplendent with joy. That she hadn't hidden her joy was what really bothered Nuria that morning.

She even wondered whether her own face would show that same rictus of defeat she'd discovered in Happy and which encouraged her to the point of wanting to be cruel to her. Perhaps Federica had also intuited a victim in her, a resentful person. Perhaps she'd discovered her envy and the thoughts of the day before, when she'd fantasized about Happy's death. In spite of everything, the other woman – the one with the spines all over her tattoo –smiled amiably at her, in a kind of solidarity in the face of a passion that Federica didn't appear to entertain. Her own desire was never to see her again. Although it was going to be difficult to forget both the woman and the electric fishes she seemed to keep within her. Unexpectedly, Nuria again saw in that woman the same sweet, calm expression she'd discovered at some point during the night. It was like being in a toboggan:

the feelings went from hatred to tenderness with no transition.

They walked down, at Nuria's insistence, but on the road which, despite being full of holes and rocks, meant there would be less distance than walking through the meadows. Happy seemed tired, and slowed down the rapid, exhausting pace that Nuria attempted to impose on her. Only Iggy followed her rhythm, going on ahead to scare birds away, and returning to demand that both the women increased their speed.

'See that? That happens to you for drinking a lot and sleeping little,' observed Nuria with malice.

But Happy didn't respond, raising her hands to her head and pressing it hard. A look of pain developed on her face and she bit her lips. Nuria ignored her and continued walking, pleasing Iggy and playing with him. Suddenly, she stopped and observed her companion, sweating and in pain. Her loose hair fell in front of her face, and she didn't bother to push it back. All the same she smiled, as she dragged her feet. Drops of sweat accumulated on her forehead and stuck to her bangs. The morning sun began to hit without compassion beyond the shade of the trees. Compassion was what Nuria was missing whenever she had Happy beside her, and she said:

'That woman yesterday, the one on the motorbike, was unbearable.'

Happy looked at her with a certain bitterness. The corners of her mouth fell, particularly accentuated by the rictus of pain that constricted her eyebrows.

'Yes, Federica, the blonde on the motorbike.'

'*Okay, darling, I know*. She's a really marvelous woman. Federica is my elder sister.'

Nuria was disconcerted. She hid the unfortunate commentary by forcing a loud laugh.

'Oh dear, forgive me. But she is so cantankerous. She loves...' And here she stammered: 'She loves attracting attention, which, if she were not your sister, would be horrendous!'

The sound of a car interrupted the conversation. Happy smiled in relief when she saw Antón's pick-up truck. She raised her hand, indicating that he stop, and Nuria looked with displeasure and disapproval at the girl's gesture. Antón was on his way to the hotel, laden with the morning's shopping: fresh fish, meat, and vegetables. When he saw Happy's pained expression, he made a half-turn and took the women to the beach, right up to the front of the building. The dog left the car and ran towards the terrace. They heard Luis's voice calling Iggy to play with him. Nuria then affectionately put her arm around Happy's waist and suggested she have an infusion of chamomile.

Happy rested her head on Nuria's shoulder and let herself be loved.

# 20

The woman, her face covered in white gauze cloth, took an apple from the dish of fruit and peeled it with a sharp knife. She remained standing, completely nude, leaning against the white tiles of the kitchen. The girl who desired her was sitting on a chair, looking at her. The woman also desired the girl, but it wasn't sufficient to possess her. No. She had to get in, rid her of her skin, and enter her flesh.

She knew what she had to do. She cut her veins and forced the girl to drink her blood. That was how she was going to produce the reunification at last, and it would be a single one in perfect silence. And the harvest moon would make sense.

Bet woke up and checked her pulse points. She wasn't bleeding. She felt enormously disappointed, but all the same she fell asleep again. The changes were coming.

# 21

Nuria's stay at the hotel did her good, apart from the intense jealousy that attacked her when she met Federica, Happy's sister. In some way, the fact that they didn't like each other wiped out that pleasant fantasy in which Happy died and she took her place, even in possessing Luis… Luis – she knew she was beginning to desire him, because Induvina's face, his soft body, were fading as the days went by, and she could barely evoke him anymore.

That Induvina was losing consistency was a good sign. She was almost convinced she'd accomplish what she'd proposed. But no. Because when she woke up, she continued rubbing her eyes to make sure the room – the things in the room – were consistent, had weight, and subjected the house to the earth. And that it continued being possessed by many people. The suspicion persisted that she had something yet to do, and the whiplashes she remembered hadn't disappeared either. And she didn't stop thinking a thousand times over about the brutal image of herself hanging from a rope with two revolvers, one in each hand, pointing at her temples. Always the same image: no variations. She did change its background, though. She didn't hang herself in her Madrid apartment, nor in Induvina's studio. Now she was doing it on the balcony of her apartment, where the whole world would see her, as if she were in a play.

But there was still another thing she couldn't manage to do. She couldn't draw. She would have been a good illustrator if she didn't leave things half done, if she didn't invest her talent in repeating geometric and floral motifs for tiles and painted paper. She would have been good at it. She recalled the creative frenzy of her adolescent days. But she also recalled when, at times, after finishing work and on sleepless nights, she'd start drawing with colored pencils and never achieve anything more than childish sock puppets. Her hands were hermetically constricted, refusing to trace anything at all that wasn't a naive scribble. A little house with a chimney, a flat meadow with round, marguerite daisies, displaying no volume. A fairy, a prince with an enormous heart on his chest. And whenever she wanted to draw and couldn't, she'd vomit. That's when she envied Bet, through the strength of her drawings, as if she painted directly with her brain or with her guts, without feeling her hands. What a marvelous talent Bet possessed, what luminosity in her madness!

However, she'd placed a table in the small room in such a way she was able to organize a studio. Something basic: the table, a kitchen chair, and a narrow bed, in which she lay down to read, to listen to the radio, or simply to rest for a while, enjoying that initial sound in which the mind begins to fantasize.

Nuria began to draw: she'd try it again. After looking attentively at the paper, she picked up a pencil and played with it on a white surface. Nothing. All she achieved were geometric lines, like those she made for the design of tiles and painted paper. Or she drew tiny flowers falling over the border of the paper. The doorbell rang, and thinking it would be Happy, she went to open the door. There was nobody there. She heard laughter that disappeared, taken away from those children who every now and then played in the corridors of the fifth floor. She waited an infinitesimal amount of time until a silence full of echoes convinced her that Happy wasn't around. She mulled over her, thinking she was a good person without any malevolence in her. She must be used to dealing with such different individuals and had become tolerant, only appearing to see the good in them. But she didn't lament offending her with that odious comment about Federica. She looked at herself in the mirror that hung over the china cabinet, imagining herself with shorter, blonde hair, with her eyes outlined in black. It was an idea, just an idea, but she liked it.

Back in the studio, she attempted a portrait of Federica. She began by leaving her mind blank, and filling it with her face. She picked up the pencil and set about drawing. When she stopped, quite a lot of time had passed and the paper was surrounded by a circular frame of portrayals of tiny chains and spines. But there wasn't a trace of Federica. Despite this, her mind was still occupied by a pair of eyes that wanted to laugh at her. She looked at the window in an attempt to erase them. Outdoors, a magpie came to rest on a eucalyptus branch, and Nuria got ready to draw it within the circular frame. She was startled to see the facility with which she moved her pencil as she drew the bird's profile. While she designed the feathers, she felt that the anxiety that had possessed her since she'd sat down was beginning to disappear. But, at the same time, she could sense something perilous about to happen, and because of that, she put a trace of terror in the bird's yellow eyes.

Time stopped in such a way she could hear the almost imperceptible movement of the eucalyptus leaves. She looked outside again and saw the magpie had become tense and was beginning to spread its wings. Just then, as its wings had almost spread and it began to take flight, a seagull threw itself upon it and savaged it in the air, letting it fall in a flutter of blood and feathers onto the balcony terrace. Nuria gave a jump when the hot drops of blood splashed her legs. Almost at the same time, a dry noise advanced along the corridor, like a thunderstorm that arrives by crossing the evening sky from the sea. Pale, shaken by the sight of the gutted magpie, she left the room hoping to see the sky clouded over the sea. But no. The sky was as luminous and as clean as that part of the house. She felt cold, and her body was as weak as it was that afternoon when *something* went through it. She trembled. Her eyes opened in horror when she noticed the glass on the paintings that covered the walls was crossed by a crack that began in the living room and continued until it fell to pieces at the end of the corridor.

She didn't understand it. She simply didn't understand what had just happened. In the middle of the confusion, she could only repeat:

'She's here, she's here.'

And the words became empty, and their meanings were diluted in the limits of the light and the shadows climbing up the broken glass.

# 22

He was strolling along the pier at the first hour of the morning. When he didn't feel too much like doing some of his kilometric walks, Vidal would arrive at the pier and talk with the sailors and with early-rising friends who still lived in the town. Since he didn't find anyone there, he decided to go into a cafeteria to have breakfast and read the paper. But again, Nuria occupied his head. There were days after he'd seen her sitting in the garden, when he couldn't stop thinking about her. She was like a headache to him. Sometimes he was sure he'd seen her looking over the building in recent years, but suddenly he threw out that absurd idea. Maybe that short-haired girl, or that other one who was around last year. But no. Or yes.

The short-haired girl lived in the building during the time when the woman on the fifth floor committed suicide, but he wasn't able to pinpoint her in any particular apartment, although it may have been on the fourth floor. He remembered her as solitary and energetic, and also, like Nuria, she spent the day swimming or walking. At some point they exchanged a few words, maybe in the elevator or on the restaurant terrace.

'At last!' he exclaimed.

He'd just clearly remembered the moment he embraced her. He recalled it with precision: they'd coincided in the elevator and she'd looked uncomfortable. But when they left the building, they encountered the woman's corpse dashed against the tiles and she, overcome, repressed a sob by hugging him, covering her mouth with his shirt, which was wet with saliva and tears. In any case, he thought it wasn't going to be easy to look closely at that girl either, who appeared and disappeared in the brief amount of time she'd spent there. He would ask Luis and Happy – maybe they would remember her. Maybe.

Since nobody he knew went to have coffee, and upset by the odd disquiet that Nuria had caused him, he decided to return to the building and do what he could to find her. She must be swimming at that hour. If he took a bus, he might arrive in time to see her emerge from the water. Outside the cafeteria he looked toward the east: the blue building stood tall at the height of the cliff. The light, already golden at this stage, gave it an enfeebled, old appearance, like the intense lights that illuminate faces and objects, merciless with the traces left by the passage of time. Vidal was inevitably fixated by these aging processes. He took his own advanced years unfavorably, by then experiencing a certain aversion for the smells he was discovering in his body which emanated a moldy odor, regardless of how often he bathed and perfumed himself.

In the almost empty bus, he sat against the last seats, near a group of boys and girls who'd be getting off at the beach with him. He didn't say so aloud, but he thought it with so much intensity that he looked around, alarmed in case someone would hear his thought:

'It smells of young people. It's the most wonderful smell in existence.'

And he sniffed as if he were inhaling the perfume of a flower.

The boys and girls got off in a gabble of happy voices, carrying knapsacks and bags of food. He left them behind, at the bus stop. Driven by the necessity to find Nuria, he increased his pace and crossed the housing development until he reached the garden that preceded the entrance to the building. He crossed over underneath the eucalyptus trees, looked out at the concrete wall with its peeling paint, from where he could see the small beach. He scanned the sea to search for a woman swimming, but there was no one in the water at that hour. He looked over at the place where Nuria usually left her towel and it wasn't there. He thought he'd arrived late, and desisted from the idea of seeing her that morning. He decided there was time to see her, while he interested himself in the state of the geraniums that were struggling to appear in the enormous round pots which, every two or three meters, climbed to the height of the balustrades.

'They're like babies' flesh, living flesh, resistant,' he thought nostalgically, and remained there, admiring the geraniums' insistence on living and the scrawny petunias that continued to bloom every year. They were weaker every time, it was true, but they were alive.

He adored flowers, but the vitality he experienced that morning, confused by the memories that came to his mind, thanks to Nuria, made him insecure in front of them. Or, more than insecure, he wanted to find within them the same energy that made plants struggle to be reborn despite the garden's obvious neglect. What he missed most about youth wasn't its beauty and smell, or its tense muscles and vibrant skin. What he missed most was the energy – something he was unable to recover no matter how many vitamins he took, how much healthy food he ate, and how much walking he did. At bottom, he accused Nuria of sublimating physical exercise (he was doing the same thing) – otherwise, if that wasn't the reason, why did she walk dozens of kilometers every day?

At that time, if Vidal adored flowers, it was for their beauty, but also because they exposed their decadence to him. He envied the energy that gave them birth and rebirth, but he also admired the lack of drama with which they shed their withered petals and let them dry at their own feet. They died without telling any more tales, and would be reborn of their own accord.

He was so carried away with the flowers that he only noticed the presence of the dog when it chewed up the strips on his sandals. Iggy liked the leather of Vidal's sandals, but it wasn't very clear to the old man whether the attraction was due to the smell of the leather, or to his ancient feet. He could hear the dog licking, and how he'd lain down on fallen leaves, curling up to have his head stroked. Vidal always thought that Iggy was true to what he expressed – he'd surrender himself for a caress. He'd never seen him with a distrustful look, or heard him give a territorial bark. Had Iggy ever barked?, he wondered. Vidal, who lived under Happy and Luis's apartment, did not remember him barking ever, not even when he was a little puppy.

'Poor, castrated thing. You're a dog, but you could have been an apple pie.'

Also, at that point, as had happened to him on the bus with the boys and girls, he looked around in case someone was listening to him. There were thoughts, regardless of how old and unbelieving he was, that generated within him an enormous insecurity. He recalled what he had told Nuria in the hotel on the mountain a couple of days ago: 'I simply observe, I no longer feel implicated.' But he knew this wasn't entirely true: he did observe, yes – but more than ever he wanted to leave proof of his presence. And, furthermore, he wanted to be a perfect person. Or almost. In that, he was also similar to Nuria.

A delicate smell wafted towards him that soon reached the intensity of a breaking eucalyptus branch. Its aroma filled the air, and to Vidal it seemed to tinge the morning a bluish green, as if an arc with a simple swath of ever-changing blues and greens had appeared above the sea and from the tops of the trees in the garden, and occupied everything.

He knew that after Iggy there always appeared Happy or Luis. He hoped it wasn't going to be Happy, because Happy exhausted him with the way she talked. In a certain way, he also felt responsible for her. He was her protector and helpmate, he knew he was obliged to take care of her. At least once a month the girl's parents phoned him to ask how their 'little one' was doing, and he informed them she continued to be a happy child.

'Good morning!' came Luis's jagged voice. Luis was a young man, but his voice sounded as if his lungs were full of bubbles and wrinkles. He smoked a lot. Vidal had told him more than once that he smoked too much, but Luis didn't seem to be worried about that.

'The flowers are alive!' said Vidal, trying to transmit his surprise at the plants' insistence on surviving.

'I saw you concentrating really hard. I looked at you and you seemed to be having an interesting conversation with the world.'

'We old folks are slaves to our fantasies.'

'And we young folks to our passion,' Luis responded, citing Vidal himself. He had heard that phrase, which Luis repeated like an homage to the old architect every time it was relevant.

They talked for a short while about the flowers and trees in the garden. Then they chatted about the state of the sea and ended up making comments about the boys and girls on the bus looking all over the beach for the best place to settle in. They selected the area best protected by the cliff, and looked around to make sure there wasn't anything preventing them from taking their first swim totally naked. Their voices climbed through the air and were so exultant, but at the same time so puritanical, that they generated tenderness.

Iggy brought eucalyptus sticks and pieces of bark. As nobody paid him any attention, he rushed around the garden as if he were out of his mind. He stopped suddenly in front of the tree trunks, sat down next to them as if expecting some type of order, and, soon after, continued with his frenetic running.

'Did you live here when the neighbor from 5E committed suicide?' asked Vidal.

Luis immediately answered no. No. No. They'd bought the apartment below, 4E, some months after the suicide.

'A girl used to live there,' he stated with precision. 'She left, that's all. Some of her things were still there when we moved in.'

'Did you get to meet her? Did you know anything about her?'

'No. We asked at the agency to see what we should do with her things, but we didn't find out where she lived and threw them away. I believe Happy kept some drawings.'

'Drawings?'

'Yes, yes. Ask Happy. I believe there was a good number of them.'

Vidal's eyes shone. He wanted to see those drawings, but, above all, he wanted to see Nuria. He said goodbye to Luis and, when he left (on the verge of losing himself among the eucalyptus trees), he asked him if he'd seen her.

'I saw her when she was returning from the hotel with Happy. That was a couple of days ago, I believe.'

'And didn't you know her from before, from other years?'

'No. I don't think so. If I saw her, I never paid any attention to her.'

Vidal ran rapidly up the stairs that led from the garden to the building, and looked up to the fifth floor.

The sky was clear of clouds, but he saw a kind of powdery litter flying about, or perhaps it was pollen from the flowers, or small insects. It wasn't very clear to him, but a light shadow blurred his view.

In Nuria's apartment, the blinds were lowered.

# 23

How sad and lonely summer is in the city. Dry, dusty, hot. The traffic had decreased considerably and the people from the local neighborhood, the ones who weren't at work or in the large stores enjoying the air conditioning, had taken refuge in their apartments until the early hours of the night dropped in temperature. Induvina doubted whether he should take his car or wait for the city bus. There was a subway entrance about two hundred meters away, but he was too tired out to walk. He had just changed his clothes, and his t-shirt was already stuck to his body, soaking from sweat. He observed the sky, the sun was beginning to reduce in size, and some fragile white clouds, high and dispersed, seemed to follow the trajectory of a reactor that reflected intense rays.

The contrails from the planes created in Induvina a childlike delight, that of a child who has just discovered something marvelous. He'd seen them and felt he had an important secret – his, only his. He'd discovered it at some moment or other. When he was little and spent time in his mother's house on the coast, he'd see the reactors' contrails and feed the dream that one day he would cross the ocean. Sometimes, when he thought a lot about it, the secret acquired the form of a little ball that he pressed between his arms. No one could see the ball, not even himself, but he really did feel it, and, with time and a great deal of concentration, he learned to find it in different places on his body. On his stomach, for example. Or in the depths of his head. When he thought about his secret, if it happened to be lodged in his guts, he felt a warm pleasure. If it was localized in his head, he could see a little ball of brilliant green floating in his cerebral gray matter. That secret made him smile like an idiot, away from the stares of others. And although with the passing years it had lost its consistency, although he could no longer remember what it consisted of, when he saw a plane's contrail he felt slightly happy.

That morning he shaved and calmly combed his hair, taking the trouble to tie it into a long braid that fell below his shoulders, but, even so, he had a dark aspect, a febrile appearance, owing to the creative passion he'd kept shut in the studio the previous week. He told himself not to think of Bet and to forget the gallery owner's humiliating visit. Even the conversation with Violeta, conducted in a hurry to do away with her things, turned into indifference, and he didn't enter her space again. A new message on the answering machine asking for Bet – that insecure, nervous voice again – deprived him a little of his tranquility, but he merely permitted himself a passing trepidation.

The first thing he was accustomed to doing when he left the studio was to go to the garbage containers. That morning he did the same thing, even though he was aware that because it was so early there'd be little to be found. It was a custom that supplied him with interesting materials for his works or for furnishing the studio. Bet liked to accompany him on those litter-retrieving expeditions, and more than once she'd found worthwhile things. The best part of it all was to go home loaded with shelves, cardboard boxes, or some minor kitchen appliance that Induvina, patiently, almost always managed to fix. The thinking sofa, which went on to preside over Bet's space in the studio, they had also salvaged on one of those expeditions. That morning, having already decided to take the city bus, Induvina arrived at the garbage containers and didn't see anything besides them. He opened them, but only found closed bags of litter, which didn't hold anything apart from organic refuse.

Carefully, with his lethargic way of walking, he went over to the bus stop. A sweaty man, seated on the bench under the shelter of the bus stop, fanned himself with the brim of a straw hat. Induvina didn't sit down. He crossed his arms over his chest and separated his legs until he found exactly the right point of balance. Then he swayed gently from one side to another, looking distractedly at the unhurried flow of the traffic.

'Do you know what time the bus to Atocha is due?' the man asked.

It was the same one Induvina was going to board. He looked at the map with the lines and hours, and confirmed it must be about to arrive.

'Maybe one passed by and I didn't see it. I'm not very attentive.'

Induvina looked at him carefully. The man adopted a pose of indifference and started to fan himself again. He was wearing a cream-colored polo shirt and gray Tergal trousers with ragged bottoms. Then he saw his shoes. They were open shoes, of worn out, brown leather. They had square toes. He looked away, but as something was attracting his attention he looked at them again, fixedly. They had a shape that seemed very familiar. But what was it? All of a sudden, a very clear image of a coffin formed in his head.

He didn't know whether the two coffins on the man's feet were a suitable, healthy image for a luminous Sunday morning in which to be especially happy. It might be a trap, because sometimes it happened that he was looking for a reason, though he might have had to search in the deepest area: a reason to become sad. Perhaps that funereal association of shoes and little caskets only occurred to prepare him for the meeting with Rubén, Bet's brother.

He paid more attention to the man. He had an ailing color – grayish, and purple circles marked his eyes. His hair, almost white, was dirty and dry.

'He looks like a cadaver' was what Induvina thought. 'A cadaver with its feet each stuck in its own little coffin.'

To get rid of that sinister image, he searched the sky for the wakes of planes. There were so many that his secret never managed to turn into any agreeable sentiment, but he caused it to disappear in a jumble of unrelated emotions: the happiness that would be in store if he finally got rid of Bet's things, and the fear of the encounter with Rubén.

Sitting on the bus, he remembered a trip with Bet. They were going home at the very last minute from their visit to the Prado Museum. It was a visit that Bet had enjoyed very much, but he, from having gone so often, no longer showed any enthusiasm, because he couldn't rely on discovering anything new. He could almost say that he'd learned to paint there, reproducing pictures, and, with time, the vision of those pieces, so often painted, became truly tedious. They bothered him, like the defects of a friend he'd known from infancy. On the return trip to the studio, also on a city bus, Bet fell asleep with her head on his shoulder. Induvina enjoyed that confiding weight, and even pushed his shoulder upward to feel the pressure of her sleeping head. Unexpectedly, Bet lifted one of his hands and began to bite one of his fingers. She bit it hard. It hurt him, but he liked it so much he allowed her, apparently asleep though she was, to continue chewing it like a cat. Immediately, she licked the same finger, then sucked it, and, finally kissed him on the mouth. They kissed each other throughout the journey, scandalously, ignoring the reproving looks of the other travelers. He even stroked her breasts and, with that bitten finger, squeezed one of her nipples until she responded to the pain by obstructing his tongue.

Recalling that moment made his hair stand on end. He shifted around on his seat, hiding an unexpected erection. At the other side of the aisle, sitting with his head leaning on the back of the seat, the old man from the bus stop shelter moved his legs, and Induvina couldn't avoid seeing the brown coffins again.

Rubén was waiting for him on a terrace near the museum. He stood up as he saw him advancing along the sidewalk and extended his hand to him.

'I'm glad to see you,' he told him.

Induvina didn't answer, he simply gave him a friendly slap on the back. They sat down. Rubén was having a whisky on ice and smoking anxiously. He was almost sure he hadn't slept. Induvina asked for a beer and drank half of it in one long, quick swig.

'What would you do if you had a twin brother and didn't know it?' asked Rubén, looking at him through his lenses with attention. He was wearing sunglasses, and Induvina couldn't see the intentions reflected in his eyes.

'If I don't know I have one, what am I going to do? Nothing!' answered Induvina with a certain annoyance.

Rubén stubbed out his cigarette and lit another. He looked backwards, inclining his head, and was quiet for a few seconds, as if thinking of something really important.

'Okay, and what if you discovered you had a twin brother you weren't aware of, what would you do?' This time he gave a satisfied smile at the question, and waited for a high-level response.

Induvina also lit a cigarette. He didn't have the slightest idea what Rubén was up to, so he decided to put an end to that idiotic string of questions.

'Look, you have to come and pick up your sister's things.'

'Hang on for a while, man. Tell me, what would you do?'

Induvina drew back the chair to gain time, and also to see Rubén's shoes. He was wearing open leather sandals. His toes had been subjected to a recent pedicure, and the nails looked as if they'd been painted in colorless polish: they were perfectly trimmed and had a brilliant opaque look. The tips of his toes reminded him of the little heads of women held down by force, bound by the straps of their sandals, and that set off in Induvina a profound sense of discomfort. But the vision he formed of Rubén's feet was totally subjective, because he knew him.

His shoes weren't coffins. They were a harem.

'If I had a twin brother, I suppose I would look for him. I don't know what to tell you.'

Satisfied with the response, Rubén lifted his glass and gave a toast in the air. A little whisky spilled over and splashed Induvina's face.

'Exactly. Well, that's what's happening to her.'

'She has a twin sister she doesn't know, and has gone looking for her?' Induvina was astounded, but seeing that Rubén seemed to be laughing at him and wasn't centered on the conversation, he thought he was pulling his leg. 'It's all the same to me whether she's searching for her twin sister or in a Buddhist sanctuary searching for herself. Either you come and pick up her things or I'll throw them out.'

Rubén became distracted every now and then, looking at the women passing by in the street and scratching his arms, pretending not to. Or he lay back on the chair as if asleep. Induvina, with a violent but concealed gesture, put an arm around his shoulders and pulled him almost close enough to rough up his cheek with his mouth.

'Either you tell me what's happening or I'll get out of here and throw everything away.'

Rubén, intimidated, became serious. He took off his glasses to rub his eyes with the palms of his hands. He had deep, gray bags under his eyes. His forehead and cheeks were full of little red dots, like mosquito bites. He scratched his arms again and, now without pretense, bent over to also scratch his ankles.

'It's the alcohol,' he confessed. 'When I drink a lot, my liver protests and I itch all over my body.'

If he was looking for some kind of compassion in Induvina, he didn't find any. He grabbed him more forcibly by the shoulder and demanded a reply.

'I'll come and fetch her things, don't worry. Tomorrow, some evening this week, I don't know... in September.'

'For sure?'

'In September, for sure. She's searching for herself, it's what you say.' He drank what was left of the whisky in one swig, called the waiter, and ordered an iced coffee. 'But listen: I've got something to tell you.'

Induvina ordered another beer and prepared to listen.

An hour later he stood up befuddled, but, in a certain way, alleviated. He put in his pants pocket a paper tablecloth with an address and telephone number that Rubén had written and re-written until his handwriting was legible. He was too drunk, despite having had one, two, or three iced coffees.

Induvina went off to his studio on foot. He'd decided to take a long stroll to think about what Rubén had just told him. He couldn't get his words out of his head, and neither could he get rid of the new obsession that had come to him that morning: feet. He looked at the feet of people walking by, and their shoes. And the more time he spent doing this, the more coffins he saw. And he saw them in pairs.

But the coffins were walking, which seemed to him a means of redemption.

# 24

She wasn't at all keen on touching the skin of peaches, it gave her the willies. She disliked biting into them without peeling them first, although peaches seemed to her like very beautiful and delicious fruit. She also couldn't stand contact with certain fabrics, such as flannel or pure wool. But what she did like was stroking apples or dog hair. At night, before going to bed, she enjoyed smoothing hydrating cream over her body – she could have spent hours with her fingers sunk into the oily, lukewarm cream, rubbing it all into her skin.

Happy had to eat a piece of fruit; she'd promised it to Luis, who was concerned about the dietary confusion of his companion. She rejected the peaches in the fruit dish and helped herself to a plum. She began to eat it in tiny little bites, as if obliged to take advantage of every little bit of red flesh she put in her mouth. She chewed it slowly, and then swallowed it. She waited a little before giving it a second bite. Her lips became wet, and a drop of juice dribbled down her jaw.

The telephone rang and she answered it, drying her hands on her thighs.

'No, I'm sorry, you've got the wrong number.'

Happy hung up and went into the kitchen. She sat down until she'd finished eating the plum, and placed the stone on a dessert dish.

The phone rang again.

'No, you've made another mistake.'

She was about to hang up, but the voice on the other end of the line retained her for a moment.

'Yes, you're right. This is the address and telephone you say, but there has to be some error.'

She hung up, shrugged her shoulders, and called Luis, who was practicing in the living room. He didn't answer. She went over to him, took off his headphones, and kissed him on the mouth. A bitter taste of tobacco was left in Happy's mouth, and Luis's was refreshed with the acid from the plum. On the amplifier connected to the guitar, the ashtray was flowing over with cigarette butts.

'Who was that?'

'I don't know. They were asking for someone called Bet.' Happy shook her head as if she'd just remembered something important, but tried to forget it by kissing Luis again.

Luis was sitting on a wooden stool, with the guitar leaning against his knees. He stood up, his t-shirt soaking wet, his forehead shining with sweat. The blinds were down, to avoid the afternoon sun heating up the living room. Even so, the heat was unbearable. Iggy was asleep on the tiles in a corner. He seemed to be dreaming, moving his legs as if he were running.

'A few days ago, Vidal asked me if he could speak to a girl who'd lived here previously. It might have been Bet.'

Happy shrugged her shoulders again. She knew Nuria had talked to her about a friend with that odd name, but she didn't feel like concerning herself with the neighbor's affairs. She'd been upset by that comment she'd made about Federica and, furthermore, there'd been something about her she'd found disagreeable. Something venomous. But she couldn't explain exactly what it was. She took the ashtray to the kitchen to empty it into the garbage, and turned on the ventilator. The sudden current threw around the papers containing musical notes that Luis had been accumulating on the table.

'Would you bring me a nice, fresh beer?'

'Okay, *darling*,' she answered from the corridor.

She stared at the ashtray as she cleaned it. She'd emptied it hundreds of times, but at that moment it attracted her attention. Perhaps she'd noticed it particularly because she heard Luis's dry cough, or because, in the darkness of the kitchen, the metal looked dull and dirty. The ashtray was a silver bowl, with two handles and a rim embossed with interlinking flowers. Luis had told her the bowl he used as an ashtray had once functioned for serving baby food. She picked up a bottle of beer, opened it with the back of a fork, making a lever on the lid, and went into the living room.

'*You know, honey?* The little bowl with which your Mommy fed you now contains the poison that's going to kill you.'

Luis ignored the comment, got under the blind, and went out to the balcony. Happy followed him. On the balcony, putting up with the sun's fierce aggression halfway through the afternoon, they shared the iced beer.

Sunday afternoon. The little beach was bubbling with people. Further away, above the trees in the garden, could be seen an upheaval on the large beach, also crammed with people, and boats with pedals and parasols. Waves of heat were forming in the air, like shining mirages. Luis pointed to the islands which, at low tide, looked brown and dry.

'Dolphins!' he shouted with the enthusiasm of a little boy.

Three dolphins were leaping in the water, keeping away from the end of the estuary. Happy, excited by the sight of the cetaceans, put her arms around his waist and her forehead against the dampness of his neck. She closed her eyes and, despite the heat, was moved by love and happiness. She kissed Luis's chest through his t-shirt.

'When I was fifteen I wrote a letter. *You know?* A letter. I wrote it to read when I was fifty.'

He didn't even look at her, but embraced her with force. He wasn't surprised at what she'd just revealed. Happy's confessions were so numerous he no longer paid them much attention. She reminded him of a little girl who described new things every second and revealed secrets to him, most of which were ingenious fantasies.

'*You know, honey?*'

'Know what?'

'Did you hear what I said to you?'

'You wrote a letter to read when you reached fifty.'

They didn't look at each other. They caressed each other over their clothes and their bodies pressed each other as if they wanted to be a single person. A planing boat appeared suddenly on the beach and caused huge waves, and the children, who were playing in the sand, shouted in protest. The tide was very low, so much so that, after the sand, you could see a greenish line of mud and algae.

'In the letter I wrote: *Dear Mrs. Happy Kuypers, I imagine you must be a happy grandmother.*'

'A happy grandmother?' Luis followed the game without showing the slightest interest.

'I didn't put exactly that, but I imagine myself that way. Like a grandmother who announces beauty creams on TV for mature skins. *Ça va?*'

Luis emitted a guffaw that hurt Happy. He entered the living room, stooping beneath the blind. Iggy continued to chase rabbits in a dream, or ran after a stick, or swam across the ocean.

It wasn't long before Happy entered.

'Do you really want to have grandchildren?'

'I'd like to have children. It was already very difficult for me to want to be a woman.'

It was a subject Luis didn't want to talk about. He didn't want to have children yet. He wanted to leave behind the delivery van, compose songs, and be successful. He wanted to travel. They'd made plans to see all of Asia and South America. It couldn't be that she was bringing up that subject again: the subject which infuriated both of them. They sat down on the sofa, and, made uncomfortable by the silence that usually preceded a huge argument, Luis turned on the TV. Happy picked up the ashtray she'd left on the amplifier, and made room for it on her lap. He lit a cigarette. He smoked calmly and extremely slowly, with the sweat dampening his skin.

Happy stroked the ashtray. Turning it around, she stroked the rim of the little bowl with her fingers. With her eyes closed, she stroked it all over, and saw her mother-in-law taking spoonfuls of purée to put into the mouth of the baby who was Luis. The perfect circular surface had become deformed, but it continued to have the cold smoothness of silver. The image of the baby in Happy's head gave way to another, radically different image: the beginnings of spring, one morning when she went up with Iggy to the hotel, taking a long walk through the wood, where they found a dead horse, its stomach burst open and covered with repulsive insects. Half the horse's body was in a large puddle that had formed with the winter rains. It was in a clearing where thousands of saffron plants were flourishing, and wild violets were climbing up the trunks of the trees.

She rubbed her eyelids to contain her rage.

'And why didn't you want to be a woman?' asked Luis, feeling obligated to do so.

'Because men don't have to give birth to babies.'

Happy's response seemed excessively puerile, but Luis didn't say anything. He loved her precisely for those incoherencies which seemed so infantile to him and, therefore, so adorable. She was his beautiful, precious little girl, delicate as a stem of rye. He could *secure* music from her just by caressing her. When he was little and lived in a village in the countryside, he would make flutes out of stems of rye. Rudimentary flutes, from which you could barely obtain two or three notes. He never forgot the taste of green, freshly cut rye in his mouth. Happy tasted of something similar to this childhood memory – she tasted of something akin to the tangible material of the first dreams he'd had while awake and already conscious of the limits of life.

Then the telephone rang. Luis got up and answered it. Happy, with the ashtray on her lap, but more attentive to the dead horse than to the baby her companion had been, paid attention to the voice, interrupted by dry, brief coughs that reached her from the end of the corridor.

'No, no. We don't know anyone by that name, I'm sorry.'

Silence.

'It's a building, man, there are lots of apartments. What d'you want me to say? The best thing you can do is sleep, and you'll soon think clearly when you wake up.'

One could hear the metallic sound of the receiver being placed on the base of the telephone. Luis's cough advanced along the corridor, amid laughter. As he entered the living room, Happy looked at him as if asking a question. He let himself fall onto the sofa, stretching out his legs until the guitar lay on the floor.

'The guy was drunk. D'you know a woman who paints?'

Happy didn't answer. There was a long silence, which the two of them measured by the filigrees sketched by the cigarette smoke in the darkness of the living room, and by the kilometers the dog ran in his dreams. Happy also measured it in children who were twins, triplets, sextuplets, in litters of babies that women gave birth to like bitches in the streets, and in the years when she wore pants and refused to appear nude before a man. If she took off her pants, if they yanked off her underwear, they'd know she was a woman, they'd penetrate her and it would hurt. Then a baby would be born, and it would be so painful her teeth would fall out and she'd go bald. Because of all this, she didn't want to be a woman.

When she was little, Happy thought that all the evils of humanity were due to the recklessness of men and women. She was convinced that if all the men and all the women in the world hid their genitals under their clothes and never went naked, the world would be perfect. Ears of corn would grow with golden, healthy grains, and not a single degenerate man would ever attempt to introduce such an ear into the body of his wife. Fresh, tasty grass would sprout, and no man would be capable of introducing either earth, the branches of trees, worms, or dead flowers into a girl's womb. That's what Happy thought when she was little.

Happy's body, deliciously dampened by the heat, caused her mouth to open and anguished breathing to begin. Luis, who'd stretched his legs over her lap, throwing the baby's little bowl onto the floor, took off his t-shirt and enjoyed the air from the fan. She was no longer thinking either of dead horses or saffron flowers. She was thinking of ears of corn and the scent of pine leaves, painful and fragrant.

'Where do you keep the drawings of the woman who used to live here before?'

'I think I put them in the attic. What do you want them for?'

'Vidal asked me about them. He also asked me if we'd known Nuria earlier.'

'No, but it seems to me that last year a weird girl lived in the same apartment,' observed Happy, not saying more.

Luis stretched out his arm and, using the tip of a finger, ran it tenderly over her lips.

'Is it true you wrote a letter?'

'*Oué*.'

'And did you write another one for me?'

'No, my love. You'll die young and beautiful.'

The silence that followed her answer was as disagreeable to Happy as if she'd bitten into the skin of a peach.

# 25

She woke up to the dull, but persistent sound of the intercom. Or rather she woke up when it had already stopped ringing. The house was dark and she thought it was still night, but when she saw the light filtering through the spaces in the blinds, she sat up with a jolt. The light was intense, golden. She noticed the lines forming on top of the bed – the tiny dots of light from the hollows in the planks. She realized she felt confused, heavy as a rock, and it was difficult for her to sit up. Her entire body hurt, as if she'd been hit really hard on her stomach, on her legs, on her arms, on the back of her neck.

She realized that not only the blinds in the room were closed. Through the door left ajar she saw the corridor – also in the dark – and was surprised because she hated the darkness. She never lowered the blinds or drew the curtains. She was there to find herself in the light. To be brilliant and luminous.

Finally she got up and let the sun into the room. She heard, as she had every day since she'd moved into the apartment, the roar of the sea, the voices of people on the beach, the children playing games in the gardens of the urbanizations. The shrieking of the seagulls put her in a bad mood. She was naked, with a fine silver chain tied around her stomach. But it was only when the chain brushed against her skin that she aware of its presence.

'No. Not again,' she murmured in resignation, too tired to even express surprise.

She looked at herself in the mirror she'd placed above the china cabinet and, feeling a sudden disgust for the naked woman she saw reflected, she tore off the chain. It fell to the floor, broken into three pieces. Then, repentant, she bent over to pick up the pieces, kissed them, and looked for the pendant.

'Where did I put it? Where did I put it? Where did I put it?' she repeated obsessively, without being able to remember a thing.

The pendant didn't appear anywhere. She was so used to the inexplicable disappearances of objects, she stopped looking for it, convinced it would appear of its own accord. But she blamed herself – yet again – for not paying enough attention to what she was doing.

As she was waking up, an intense pain in her arms made her look at them carefully. That was when she became a bit scared: she discovered scratches on her pulse points, and on her right hand a profound burn beginning to form a scar. Her knuckles were also crossed by small but deep cuts, as if she'd been breaking glass with her fists. The cuts left traces of blood between her nails and her fingers. She didn't know, either, how she'd come by the scratches, the burn, or the cuts. For a moment she thought maybe she'd invited someone to spend the night with her, so she began to prepare herself to look all over the house for the remains of a possible visit, perhaps a violent lover.

But no.

She covered herself in a bathrobe and, alert, with all her senses wide awake, she began to look for a rational explanation for what had occurred in the apartment. She noticed the smell of rancid meat and went into the kitchen. On the table was a plate with the leftovers of roasted meat, and the oven door was ajar. She didn't remember anything, but when she saw the oven she understood the burn on her hand. She looked at it, thinking she must have been burned by the electric bars of the grill. At the sight of little scarabs beginning to form, she calculated they must have spent at least a couple of days for the blister to turn to crust. If that's how she had burned herself – by roasting the meat.

'But who could have brought meat to the house? Meat, meat, meat...' she asked herself obsessively.

There was a pile of cigarette butts accumulated in a glass of water. The water had a brownish color and the butts had fallen to bits. She also discovered two empty, squashed packets of cigarettes under the kitchen table.

As if someone had thrown them against the wall and they'd fallen to the floor after their impact on the white tiles. An aftertaste of tobacco and acidic wine, and the mixed saliva in her mouth, made her think she had drunk and smoked. On the table-top there was a bottle of rather expensive wine. The bottle was empty.

'Shit, I shouldn't drink,' she said in a loud voice to anyone who could hear her, punishing herself with a slap. It hurt her so much she pressed her hands on her face so her tears wouldn't spill out.

But even so, after blaming herself for drinking, she calmed down a little. She didn't remember anything, but there was an explanation for that: it wasn't the first time alcohol had prevented her from remembering.

She pulled up the blind, opened the door that led to the balcony, and a stench of rotting meat caused her to feel nauseous. On the floor, exactly in front of the door to the small room that had been furnished as a studio, a huge number of blue flies and other insects had installed themselves on the cadaver of a bird. A yellowish, viscous liquid traced out a little puddle of thick blood.

'The seagull!' she exclaimed as, restraining her need to vomit, she entered the kitchen again. Her throat itched and she was thirsty.

She remembered the magpie she'd seen perched peacefully on the branch of the eucalyptus and the seagull that degutted it. She recalled that and the explosion which, like a thunderclap, had gone through the apartment's corridor. She went outside and saw the broken paintings, but they hadn't broken in the way she remembered. It wasn't a crack crossing the glass and becoming ever bigger with the distance it covered from the living room. No. What she saw was the glass broken to pieces as if someone had punched them with their fists or with some heavy object. She looked at her mangled fingers and didn't take long to establish a convincing connection.

She began to tremble, but from worry, not fear. Extreme pallor had covered her face, and she bit her lips to the point of pain. She wanted to feel pain. Her hands were trembling, a drop of blood sweetened her mouth.

'At least I can explain this. Okay, I drank too much, I shouldn't have had anything at all,' but she didn't want to think about how she'd procured the wine. Or the tobacco. At that point, her thought process whirled around and around and came up against an enormous complexity that lost itself in profound darkness.

She should go into the living room. She breathed deeply before she did so, waiting a while before arming herself with sanity prior to crossing the threshold. The living room was dark. The light coming from the room and the kitchen diminished the total darkness. The light didn't even filter through the blinds in the living room, which had been carefully closed.

When she entered, her bare feet hesitated over something soft, which sank with every step. It was like a spongy carpet. She crossed the living room, opened the blinds and was then surprised at what was in front of her: the floor was covered in tiny bits of paper. There were thousands and thousands of tiny bits of paper. Drawing paper, newspaper, toilet paper, paper tablecloths. Her heat beat quickly and she found it difficult to breathe. How was it possible? Where had all those papers come from? The flight of a fly, which was making circles around her head, irritated her so much she got hold of a ceramic vase and threw it at it. That was stupid, because the fly buzzed with greater energy and the vase smashed when it reached the floor under the table. Right under the table was where there was a greater accumulation of little bits. But there was also an empty space, as if someone had sat there. The papers surrounded that empty area.

She didn't understand it.

The fly, which was trying to get to the burn on her hand, kept on and on piercing her ears and head. Sometimes it got so near her body she felt as if the movement of its wings tickled her skin without touching it. She wanted to kill it, thumping and twisting it until her nerves were distended. She would hit it, hang it, pass it through a guillotine, shoot it full of bullets, burn it alive, and she'd enjoy hearing its sickening fly screams, just to feel better.

Once, some time ago, she subjected herself to a session of hypnosis with the sole intent of curing insomnia. As she was a very curious person, she felt very much as if she wanted to try therapy of that sort. More than for curing insomnia, as they'd promised her, she did it to know what it felt like, and because perhaps she could discover more about herself. Perhaps she would learn why she had those suggestive fantasies in which she appeared lying in a primitive bed with a baby at her side, or why she saw herself playing on a mountain of red mud while she ate an appetizing fruit. She had the illusion that the hypnosis would take her to one of those moments, and then she could affirm she was aware of having lived from the beginning of humanity. Or, at least, she was aware of an existence in a collective memory which, from time to time, manifested itself to her with details so precise they were disquieting.

But that didn't happen. The hypnotist asked her to lie down on a really comfortable gurney. He covered her in a light wool blanket because, from what he explained to her, body temperature drops during hypnosis and she'd feel cold. He told her he was going to count backwards, and then play some relaxing music. She let herself be guided, counting on being transformed into a tiny being floating among the stars. Or within a millet seed. But no.

When she was at the point of surrender, she heard the sound of waves on the sea, and became worried. She started to move around under the blanket, to become tense, as if placing herself on guard before *something* was going to happen. She squeezed her fists and bit her tongue. Shortly after that, the flight of a bird brushed her body, then another, and another, and another, until after those flights came the shrieking of the seagulls.

'No. No. Not seagulls!' she protested, but the hypnotist didn't seem to hear her, or, as nothing like that had ever happened to him before, he believed she wasn't sufficiently asleep and insisted on counting backwards. Three, two, one.

'Relax.' He almost told her off.

She had become so exasperated with the seagulls' shrieks that she got up and began to lash out at him. Then, searching for a way out, she broke the glass in one of the windows. She needed to get away from that place – she couldn't avoid it. She couldn't stay there for another second, with the seagulls attacking her.

Of course, Nuria knew this because she'd been told about it.

The buzzing of the fly, which she ended up squashing with a slap on her own face, brought to her one of those scraps of memory that were so distressing: she saw herself sitting under the table, crying and tearing up with her hands and teeth the sketchbooks she'd bought, the newspapers she'd borrowed every day at the restaurant, while she surveyed a mountain of rolls of toilet paper with the same satisfaction of that primitive baby that was breastfeeding from her.

She gave in, seated on the sofa with her knees up, her elbows on her knees, and her head hidden in her arms. With every finger of her two hands pressing the back of her neck, she adopted the consistency of a stone. She was afraid – terrified – but at least she knew the disaster she'd met up with at the apartment when she woke up might have a rational explanation.

What seemed not to have any rational explanation was the presence of the woman in an iridescent swimsuit, angrily staring at her from the corridor.

'The house is very dirty,' she yelled at her, and her voice reached Nuria some instants after the woman's mouth moved.

And neither was there any rational explanation for the stains on the wooden floor, which gave off greasy, sticky blood, and didn't smell any longer of lettuce salad but of an open wound.

And neither was there any convincing explanation for the children's voices echoing through the walls of the entire house.

She ran out of the living room and locked herself in the small room. She looked for the pendant to press it and abate her fear, but couldn't find it. She didn't know what she'd done with it, though it wouldn't take too long to discover it. It turned up among the jumbled sheets, when she stretched them to tidy up the bed a little. When she saw it, she understood the use it had given her and why she had never been separated from it. It smelled of sex, of her own sex. She put her hand on her stomach and could still feel the tremor of her last orgasm.

She longed to get out, she tried to get out, but something in the house trapped her and she felt the same exhaustion as the days previously. Something, inside there, pronounced her name in an affectionate, charming tone, like when her brother Rubén soothed her to sleep: *Until tomorrow, good night, sleep well, goodbye.*

Despite the terror, she fell profoundly asleep.

## 26

The tiny creature was snatched out of the peace in which it unconsciously floated, and manifested itself as a cloth of white gauze covering the face of a woman. It was the hand of that very woman that removed the cloth, and her face took on the form of a leopard's head, the vertebral column of a tyrannosaurus, the eyes of a hyena, it was the scent of rose-apple, barbed wire, yellow dress, football, peach, light, green, acidity, song. Iodine. Nothing.

The tiny creature returned to its shelter, horrified and tired, very tired. And Bet decided it was time to wake up.

## 27

He walked along the bay for half an hour, following the band of algae and gray sand left by the tide. He hurt his foot on a sharp decline and turned around towards the rocks that separated him from the large beach at the other side of the pine grove. He was waiting for Nuria. This time around she wasn't going to escape; he needed to talk to her because he could intuit *something* strange. But no. He couldn't tell exactly what that *something* was. It wasn't eight o'clock yet and he was already there: he wasn't going to let her get into the water without talking to her first. And she didn't appear. He looked towards her apartment and the blinds were still closed. He'd wait a little longer before pressing the intercom again. He'd spent almost a week pressing that bell several times a day, to no avail. Nuria never answered. She didn't go down to dinner at the restaurant, and neither did she go out for walks with Happy. But no, that wasn't a hundred percent true: he'd seen her one afternoon carrying shopping bags, absent, lost, and sad, gray, lifeless... as if ill. It didn't seem like a good moment to approach her, but it worried him even more, and, seeing her in that condition, his obsession increased.

He walked around on the sand, as clumsily as Iggy, always returning to the spot where Nuria usually left her towel and the little bag with her keys and pendant. 'Why would the pendant be so important to her?' Vidal wondered. But that morning, on that little bit of sand where Nuria's belongings usually were, a young couple had sat down to talk. They had finished there, right on top of Nuria, their night of drinking on the town.

'You and I have something very special, I've always known that,' he was saying, holding on to a bottle of vodka. When he pronounced the word 'special,' there was no doubt he was telling the girl he wanted to have sex with her.

But the girl, serene, and more enthusiastic about being at the beach so early, more focused on the marvel of a new dawn than on the drunken lad accompanying her, resisted him.

'I've always known there's something special between us.'

'Yes, of course there's something special – my sister, you jerk! You're her boyfriend, or did you forget that by drinking too much?' She pushed him away with the tips of her fingers, as if fearing to soil herself by contact with him.

'But between you and me there's something... you know? There's something.'

'Not again! Why don't you be quiet for a little while, just a little while?' The girl pushed him, and he fell onto the sand, without losing his hold on the bottle. She stood up and went over to the water, rolled up her pant legs, and played with the waves. She washed her face and wet her hair. Meanwhile, the lad tried to take a last swig of the vodka, but the empty bottle struck him in the teeth.

'Shit!' he protested, collapsing half unconsciously.

Vidal got out his camera and photographed them, furtively. The girl had just got into the water and was bathing in her clothes. He couldn't avoid taking the photos. He was still a compulsive collector: he didn't accumulate objects, but he did images. He must have used up at least half a roll of film. As he needed to give a solid name to the box where he had to keep it, he approached the girl, and, assuming she wouldn't respond, asked her:

'What's your name?'

'María. Why?' Dripping, the girl stood up.

'No reason. Just to know your name. And what's your companion called?'

'That imbecile?'

'Yes, the one who hangs on to the bottle when he sleeps.'

'It's Martiño, Martiño Gómez. Put him where you like, the whole world will know he's a jerk.'

Vidal smiled with satisfaction. When he arrived home he took the roll from the camera, put it away in the box, and wrote on it: 'María and Martiño Gómez at the beach. August 30th, 1992.'

Entertained with his unexpected haul of images, Vidal forgot he'd been there because he was waiting for Nuria. And Nuria hadn't appeared. He looked at the apartment again, and the blinds were still closed. He then noticed Luis's bougainvilleas. The flowers had lost their colors and the Republican flag was resisting fading and dying. It was a sign that August was coming to an end and that Nuria would leave. She might have already abandoned the apartment without saying goodbye to anybody, something that he didn't find strange. Even so, he went up to the apartment, pressed the bell and waited. Nothing.

Vidal knew that, with her silence, he would miss his last opportunity to love. He was saddened.

## 28

Something, *inside*, prevented her from abandoning the apartment. She tried to leave, but no. She'd fallen into a deep sleep. When she woke up, she didn't understand what had happened to her. She'd gone through the euphoria of knowing she was far away and free, because she'd controlled her feelings, because of self-control, exhaustion, satisfaction, apathy. And, unexpectedly, she felt a new sensation she hadn't remembered from before: fear.

She secluded herself in her room and only left, walking really close to the wall, when she couldn't avoid going to the bathroom. The house continued in an absolute mess and the woman in the swimsuit appeared to her everywhere. She also saw new faces reflected in the mirror: a young girl with short, blonde hair, looking similar to Federica, but she also saw another, more aggressive, with an orange mane. She recognized them as strangely familiar, but didn't know why. And when she had no option but to go to the bathroom, she closed her eyes so she wouldn't see them.

During the four, five or maybe six days she spent locked in the house, she had several calls on the intercom. She didn't answer any of them, aware they might be from Happy, worried about her disappearance. She didn't want anyone to see her like that, but the house didn't permit her to answer those calls either. It exercised absolute control over her, and she behaved like a surrendered prisoner, lacking the strength to resist.

Suddenly, someone rang the doorbell and knocked insistently at the door. After two knocks, the person called her name. She recognized Luis's voice and took advantage of that intrusion to look for a way out – a saving hand.

'Hey, Nuria! Are you there?' Luis's voice was insistent, assertive, as if he were ready to bring down the door if she didn't respond.

This time, embarrassment overcame the fear of knowing she was trapped, and she only opened the door a bit so Luis would leave as soon as possible.

'Your face looks awful, woman!' Luis didn't hide his surprise. He tried to get in, but she thwarted him. 'What on earth have you done to your hair?'

Nuria raised her hands to her head. Amid her long mane she had some rough, uneven locks that grazed her ears.

'I'm okay. I've got the flu, that's all. The flu.'

Luis stepped back from the door, driven out by a malodorous smell whose source he couldn't distinguish: did it come from Nuria or from the apartment? She looked at him in desperation. It wasn't very clear to him if she was asking him to buzz off at once or begging for help.

'This morning some guy named Induvina called you, asking after you and a friend of yours – Bet, Betty – something like that. Another dude also called some days ago, asking for your friend.' He spoke rapidly, and as soon as he'd said what he had to say, he gave a half-turn to leave, but still insisted on asking her if she was well.

'Yes. I'm sorry they bothered you.' Nuria said goodbye and slammed the door.

She looked at herself in the mirror and discovered the disaster she'd made of her hair. Not only was it damaged by cuts with a knife, it was also discolored, almost white, as if it was the hair of a doll. She had no idea why her hair was like that, though she soon found the black locks scattered all over the house as well as several bottles of peroxide in the bathroom. By then she wasn't worried. Simply knowing that Induvina (and maybe also Rubén) had called her encouraged her to make some kind of a decision. She also felt a little more tranquil because they'd asked for Bet, because if Bet had been there, she was sure to have been guilty of the disorder and the meat and the tobacco and of her lamentable state.

'Damned bitch!'

She went directly into the small room, certain she was going to find some trace of her friend there. And she wasn't mistaken: the walls were covered in meaty, vibrant jellyfish, sketched in variously colored chalk, scattered on the floor and on the table. They seemed alive, the jellyfish. Their tentacles moved in the air in an attempt to capture her. Strangle her. Squeeze her. Hang her. Fragment her again, debilitating her.

'Damned bitch!'

There was a note on the table written in a large, open hand, like the waves of a fearsome sea: 'When you wake up, I'll be gone. Don't get too angry. Bet.'

Nuria curled up on the floor, her back pressed against the lintel, and burst into tears. Everything hurt so much, inside. She was so tired, and so disappointed, because Bet had found her again, because she thought it impossible to acquire the strength to flee from the voices in the apartment, from that irrevocable attraction that prevented her from even leaving her room. She went over what she wanted to be, and only wanted to be her own self, inimitable, to live without all those voices in her head, to be free.

To be free. Without limits: that's what she wanted. And then she pressed the pendant and, like a revelation, it showed her the moment when Induvina had given it to her. On its top was a little cover with a diamond on it, as if it were a bottle of perfume. She ran to the room and recovered the silver chain she'd broken into pieces some days ago, and realized she ought to have kept it inside the pendant. And she also realized that the chain was a dyke, a retaining wall, a limit that helped her not to disperse herself like millet seeds all over the universe.

She sucked up the tears that had gotten into her mouth, remembered Induvina's phone call, and, though she looked calamitous, decided to get out of that place. She got dressed, covered her hair with a cap advertising the restaurant, and flung herself out of the apartment.

It was still early, it can't even have been midday.

## 29

She dialed Induvina's number and leaned against the bar, covering her face with her hand to disguise how bad it looked. She waited for one, two, three tones, until she heard a woman's voice at the other end of the headphone, which couldn't possibly be Bet's. This hurt her, but in less than a second, while the woman asked who was calling, Nuria decided she couldn't hang up.

'Is Tomás there?'

'He's busy. Who's speaking?'

'Tell him this is Nuria. I want to talk to him.'

Silence. Absolute silence, except for the other woman's breathing.

'He can't come to the phone. I'll let him know you called.'

The sound of a telephone being hung up.

Berta, the waitress, looked at her inquisitively out of the corner of her eye. Nuria paid for the call and left the restaurant.

The children from the urbanization all seemed to be reunited that morning, playing football in the middle of the street. The girl in the yellow dress was also playing. She was agile and quick with the ball, but it looked as if the other kids ignored her. She gave the impression she was playing a different game from the others, a game played independently, in which she was the only participant. Nuria raised her hand to greet her, to make that moment real. And, as she raised her hand, she saw the scar from the burn. It had developed between her thumb and index finger and looked like the crater of a volcano. She didn't like that image – so dramatic and authoritative – and changed it for a pink anemone opening up in the water. It was an image more suitable for a sunny morning at the end of August.

Two women, wearing light summer dresses, were seated on wicker chairs on the sidewalk in front of the supermarket. In reality, to Nuria's eyes, they were floating above the sidewalk as if they were about to disappear. They greeted her when she passed by, and one of them, without getting up but in an affectionate tone, as if she'd maintained some previous conversations that Nuria wasn't aware of, said to her:

'You look so much better today.'

Nuria looked around to see if she was speaking to someone else and not to her. But there was nobody else there, only herself and those two women sitting on wicker chairs. She felt uncomfortable, but didn't want to be discourteous.

'Thank you,' she said, inclining her head a little, trying to hide her lying amiability.

The woman took hold of her hand.

'The cream did you good! It's almost cured!', and she ran the tip of her finger over the burn.

Nuria was alarmed. She withdrew her hand, took her leave, and left with a hurried gesture.

'Look after yourself, little one,' she heard the woman's voice say as she walked off.

The vertigo again. But not physical vertigo, as if she were about to fall from the top of a mountain. She hadn't experienced that kind of vertigo for a long time. The fact of perceiving space in that special, inconsistent way had obliged her to become aware of her body and, above all, her feet. She knew her feet were well placed on the ground: she could never fall. She couldn't even fall from a table, or a balcony, or from the top of a mountain. It was a simple matter of logic, and she had to review that basic logic so as not to lose her balance all the time.

The vertigo that disquieted her at that moment had to do with her way of feeling. It was as if all the spheres that stored up her time had exploded and dragged her holograms along with them. Time had been threshed like an ear of corn. The holograms flew through the air and an enormous hole formed at the very center of her body that seemed to attract all the universes with their mirrors, their bowls and straight lines. An emotional storm attacked her: she heard voices so strong they wounded her eardrums; she saw the trees on the beach as if they were giants and then dwarves; the sea flew and then the sky was the sea; the tips of her fingers hurt her because the air stabbed them like pins. The worst of it was the smells, because she discerned all of them, from the children's sweat to the nauseous stench of the magpie rotting on the balcony.

But it must have all happened in a fraction of a second because, when she looked again for a point of reference so as not to be dragged off by the vertiginous spiral, she saw the women sitting in their wicker chairs, and clearly heard the one who'd stroked her burn say to her:

'Look after yourself, little one,' as she said goodbye with a smile.

Calmly, she took a breath of air. A gentle aroma of pine and eucalyptus brought her back to life. She noticed the bushes of marguerite daisies in flower in front of the abandoned houses. She caressed them to make sure the furious wind that had swept away her senses a short time ago had disappeared. A delicate softness brushed her fingers as she touched the petals.

How distant her apartment seemed to her then, so cold, so gray, and so hostile!

Little by little she recovered her tranquility, and even gave a pleasant smile when she came across Vidal.

'I've been searching for you for days,' said the photographer. 'I thought you'd already left.'

'Good. No, I'd gone out,' answered Nuria, avoiding explanations, though she remembered telling Luis she was ill and corrected herself. 'The flu, yes, I had the flu.'

'I rang the doorbell,' Vidal seemed worried. 'I rang the doorbell several times. I waited for you on the beach...'

'I went out for a walk. Now...'

'I have to talk to you.'

'Not now, please.'

Vidal simply couldn't understand why that girl became so nervous when she saw him, why she got so upset when he longed to hold her and caress her. He couldn't recall ever having done anything to make her feel uncomfortable. He focused on the burn in her hand, the little cuts on her knuckles, and the scars from scratches crossing her pulse points, which she'd attempted to hide under the long sleeves of her sweater. He also noticed she wore a different expression from two days previously. When he saw her at Happy's hotel, her gaze shone and she had a luminous expression. When he found her sitting in the garden, she was calm and delightfully beautiful. Now, however, she reminded him of the night when he'd found her in the restaurant at the beginning of August, with wrinkles marking her brow, her eyebrows crumpled and exhausted. But she didn't appear to be tense, on the verge of exploding, as she had been that night. Actually, quite the contrary, it was as if she'd already exploded, and the suffering had deposited on her face a dark sediment of dirt. And, aware of this, Nuria was lowering her gaze to hide it.

Vidal was moved by an unexpected tenderness.

'Are you okay?' he asked her.

She was in such a weak state, she was so fragile, it was difficult for him to hold back a sob. But it didn't take her long to recover, and she limited herself to responding that she was in a hurry.

'I have some photographs of you,' Vidal told her.

She had begun to walk, but turned around and, without any pretense, looked at him with annoyance.

'Photographs?' Her voice had a sharp, injurious tone.

'Yes, photographs,' Vidal was shocked by that irate utterance. 'Well, I believe it's you. They were taken some years ago.'

Nuria was going to deny any possibility of his having taken any photographs of her whatsoever. But then she saw the apple tree.

The apple tree was old, its trunk half decayed. It stood behind the ramshackle fence of one of the last little houses in the urbanization. It was one of those abandoned houses, the garden and orchard jam-packed with weeds and a pair of fruit trees: a fig tree strangled by brambles and also the old apple tree. But on the apple tree there was some red fruit. Nuria noticed one of the apples was about to fall, and, in the delicate tension of the stalk connecting it to the tree, she recognized the tension and the fragility with which she perceived life.

She became emotional at the sight of the fruit about to fall.

'I'm sorry,' she apologized, and her voice became friendly, almost sweet.

And then, as if it were not herself who was speaking, she agreed to meet the photographer at the restaurant in the middle of the afternoon. Yes, she wanted to see the photos, even though she assured him it was totally impossible that it was she being portrayed. She'd never been there. Well, she'd been there as a child, but that was so long ago now, it was impossible he'd recognized her.

As she walked towards the town, without being very sure where she was going, she came across the hairdressing salon where she'd had her hair washed the evening she arrived. A sudden desire obliged her to go in. There were two clients at the sinks and another awaiting her turn. The young man who'd attended to her that time received her with a certain lack of interest.

'We can't see to you for another hour.'

But then the woman who appeared to be the owner of the salon and who was washing the head of one of the clients approached her, almost laughing.

'How long it's been!' And she kissed her. 'I knew you'd come back! Are you in the same apartment as ever?'

'Yes,' answered Nuria, by now not showing any emotion, let alone surprise, as if she knew there was no sense in opposing what was about to happen. 'Yes. I want to have my hair cut shorter, and have it dyed...'

Ashamed, she removed the cap from her head. She was worried what that solicitous and cheerful woman would think of her, as she looked at her in surprise and held back a laugh.

'What a crazy thing you did to your hair, dear! But what did you put on it?'

‘It doesn’t matter. Can you fix it?’

‘Do you want the color you had before? You looked gorgeous!’ The woman, with an almost intimidating enthusiasm, got hold of Nuria by the arm and took her over to a panel covered in photos.

With the tip of a long nail, a tiny bit chipped and painted in deep red, she showed her a girl with short, very untidy hair. And blonde, very blonde, almost white. The girl’s eyes were outlined in black pencil and were very dark. Her smooth, pronounced cheekbones highlighted her slender face. Nuria reacted with the indifference of someone who doesn’t remember what she’s being accused of, and smiled with childlike innocence. Even so, on seeing her, she recalled Happy’s sister, and wanted to be exactly the same: challenging, self-confident, and insulting with so much passion. Just like Federica, the girl in the photo had a fiery gaze.

‘Yes, like before,’ she decided.

‘I took this photo of you here about four or five years ago,’ the hairdresser said, putting on a nostalgic tone. ‘How time flies! But come on, dear, it’s going to take us a couple of hours to leave you looking like that.’

Halfway through the afternoon, Nuria went up the slope to the urbanization, walking so rapidly that her lungs hurt. She wanted to get to the apartment. She wanted to get to the apartment and open the envelope she’d left on top of the china cabinet with the photograph in it. She needed to see it. She entered the house, not even shutting the door. She opened the envelope, took out the photo, looked at herself in the mirror and trembled in panic. She straightened her legs, searching for the security of the floor, but realized the territory of fear is similar to that of dreams: there's no firm land on which to dig in one's feet.

## 30

He rested his head on the glass window pane and looked at the lights that were on at the other side of the avenue. Night had fallen just a short time ago. During the last hour, low, stormy clouds had passed by, which let fall some misleading rays and wet the streets with sad, useless rainfall. The glass panes in the studio were wet and fresh; one could see the drops sliding down them with unbearable inertia until they disappeared, absorbed by the dried-out wood of the window.

He turned and saw Violeta clearing the table. She was a good girl, but Induvina wasn't too keen on the attitude she'd displayed over the past weeks. He wanted to be alone and work without anyone roaming around the studio. He wasn't exactly an ungrateful person, but it so happened he asked Violeta to buy him a baguette, and she ended up cooking for him the whole month. He'd asked her for a small favor, and she wouldn't stop jumping gratefully around him just because he'd asked it of her. She was fantastic. She was always there, willing to lend a hand. She only disappeared when Induvina fell in love and another woman came into his life. It was then that Violeta would start up a new love relationship of her own, ending it when he ended his. Induvina didn't realize Violeta started and ended her relationships at the same time he did. He discovered this when he took his forehead away from the glass and his headache came back, excruciatingly. At that precise moment, as she cleared the table, he saw her so devoted and happy washing the brushes, cleaning out the ashtrays, and setting out a vinyl print tablecloth, that it made him feel ashamed of himself and also of her.

Violeta had been there for the past three weeks while he painted. She cooked and cleaned up the studio, making sure there was cold beer in the refrigerator, and nursing back to health a dying plant into which Bet would cruelly dump the dregs of the gin and tonics she enjoyed drinking in the evening.

'I promise you they do it good!' she would say, laughing. 'Wicked living suits everyone. See how handsome you look, and you take such little care of yourself!'

Poor Violeta. She was too obsequious for him to even desire her. He didn't want complacency, but constant stimulation, even when it did him so much harm that in the end he needed to resort to the tranquility offered by Violeta or by drugs. He decided that the best thing to do would be to talk to her, but he'd tried to talk to her so many times that he waited in silence, with a gesture of sorrow and cowardice, for Violeta to place a bag of hot hamburgers on the vinyl tablecloth and open it.

They were from the neighborhood burger joint, where he ate more times than were recommendable. The smell of the meat and the fried potatoes opened his appetite and he even felt a touch of joy. She offered him a cold beer.

'Isn't it time yet for you to get rid of her things?'

'No. Rubén told me to wait until September. That's what we agreed.'

'You're a fool, Tomás.'

'There's no rush. There's a time for everything.'

'You're stupid, Tomás.'

After speaking with Rubén half a month previously, one Sunday morning when he found coffins at the feet of every human who crossed his path, Induvina called Bet. Rubén had written an address and a phone number on a napkin. He phoned her that same afternoon, but was told Bet didn't live there. He tried again to no avail. He decided it was best to forget her and keep painting. He hadn't left the studio for fifteen days, also waiting for the woman who asked for Bet to call. But no. That woman didn't call and he couldn't forget Bet, so he spoke to Rubén again.

'I'm sure she's there. Why don't you ask for Nuria Uría? If Nuria's there, Bet could show up at any minute.'

He dialed the number that very morning and was startled when a man's voice answered, telling him he knew Nuria and would give her the message. He was delighted and waited by the phone the whole day. But no, it didn't ring. At least he didn't hear it. Maybe Violeta didn't allow it. Maybe.

Looking at Violeta while they ate, he thought of the times he'd shared a meal with Bet. She loved meat, enjoyed roasted meats. She liked good wine, and had a discriminating palate. She was nothing like Violeta, who was sitting at the other side of the table, biting into the hamburger, holding it as though fearful of staining herself with it, wiping her lips after each mouthful.

But yes, Bet was like Violeta at times, proper and conscientious, even apathetic and sad. Looking at the woman across from him, fearful of getting grease on her hands, Induvina wondered how it could be possible for someone to completely forget a moment lived with such intensity? This happened with Bet. She was there and not there. She was tenderly cruel and suddenly a lifeless body, indifferent, apathetic. She felt and ceased to feel. She greedily sought his caresses and suddenly his caresses irritated her. She would even forget her own name. She would bang the wall while asleep, clawing at herself, kicking and not believing him when he told her she looked like someone else. Induvina would move away from her when these things happened. He would simply watch her pass through the studio door and not reappear until days later, happy and radiant... Bet once again. Rubén would attempt to explain his sister's transformations, but Induvina wouldn't believe him. He couldn't understand it. In fact, when he returned to the studio after speaking with him, he looked among her things once again to understand the situation, and what he thought was that the siblings were hoodwinking him again. But only Bet was there. Bet at the work table, in her books, in her sketches, in the computer, in the music, in the lipstick-stained cigarette butts, in the bits of paper she would tear and tear and tear, as if searching for the means to rearrange an image incorrectly put together. As if arranging herself.

That mania Bet had for tearing up paper! She would fill everything with torn papers that she would later rearrange into lovely images, as if to make a mural. For example, she would tear up the silver foil lining of an ounce of chocolate to make ephemeral jewelry with which she would adorn her body for him. And he, poor Induvina, couldn't keep up with her at times. He was scared when she opened the trunk packed to the brim with sex toys. It frightened him to see how she would transform herself for him, clad in leather and metal, and how she would spin like a top, ecstatic and free like the pain that possessed her, and caused her eyes to glow with a fire that could only be extinguished by taming her, possessing her, setting boundaries for her. So he let her make herself up, dress as she pleased, show him her fierce desire, and turn into an animal in rut, available and demanding. And yes, they would end up making love in a brutal fashion, for hours and hours to the point of exhaustion, until their skin was rubbed off and their bodies were bone dry.

Who was he to limit her? Even if Bet wanted him to be a sort of retaining wall, who was he to limit her? He wasn't going to reject her charm, her talent, the devastating pleasure they enjoyed. After all, he was aware that to Bet he was just another paintbrush in her own hands – a mere instrument. Nothing more. He gave much thought to how he could offer her something to help her when she was unbridled. He thought of giving her a pendant containing a hidden chain. So she'd know that if she wanted to, she could tie herself to him. The chain and the pendant. These were his thoughts when an irritated Violeta interrupted them.

'Who's Nuria?'

Induvina looked at her but didn't know how to answer. He then regretted not having spoken to her.

'Do you have a new girl?' Violeta asked him. 'You can tell me if that's the case. It's not all that hard.'

Violeta put on the plate the piece of hamburger she was about to eat, and turned instead to picking up French fries and dipping them in ketchup. She was no longer as happy as when she was setting the table. She wasn't humming anymore. She was waiting for an answer, but Induvina remained silent. He seemed completely absent.

'She called you an hour ago, and it isn't the first time. You're not aware of anything, Tomás. You don't see me and you don't hear the phone ring, you're not even worried about... You're damned selfish.'

'Did Nuria call?'

Violeta got up, offended by his sudden awakening of interest. She wiped her mouth and tidied up the table. When she was done, she put her things in a valise and left.

Induvina saw her little body disappear from the studio as well as her domestic disposition, and was glad she'd left. He could hear the sound of the door as it closed. He stood up and looked for a trace of Nuria in the space Violeta had occupied in recent weeks, in the places she'd fought to clean and put in order. But no, he didn't find anything other than the folder with drawings of tiles.

Oddly enough, he stopped being interested in Bet and began thinking about Nuria.

# 31

Happy spent the day asleep. Luis tried to wake her up when he came down from Nuria's apartment, but desisted when he saw her looking so peaceful, with the bag of dry ice she'd put on her forehead having fallen on her pillow. He picked it up and put it away in the freezer.

She had a terrible headache that morning. She got up for lunch, went out with Luis to take Iggy for a walk, and, shortly before noon, decided to go back to bed. At six in the evening, she appeared in the living room, like an almost transparent ghost. Her face didn't look good, she closed her eyes because the light distressed her, and Luis rushed to lower the blinds. She lay down on the sofa. He rescued the bag of ice from the freezer and put it on her forehead.

'Listen, your friend was looking like shit. She wouldn't let me in and she stank like a corpse.'

'She's a bit strange. She told me she saw holograms.'

'And what's that?'

'I can't explain that to you now.' Happy stretched her legs and twisted her mouth.

'Does it still hurt you?'

She didn't reply. She picked up her right hand and nibbled at it. It itched. She changed her position, but soon stood up. She was really trashed.

'I'm going to lie down again.'

Luis observed her as he took off along the corridor. She seemed to be dragging her right leg slightly.

'*Ça va?*' he asked her. 'Do you want us to go to the doctor?'

Before she entered the bedroom, Happy raised her hand and waved goodbye.

'*Ça va,*' she said, in Donald Duck's voice. He smiled and stopped worrying.

Shortly after Happy went to bed, he went to see her and covered her up to her chest in a sheet, kissed her lips, and shut the door. He went back to the living room, rolled up the blinds, and went out to the balcony.

It was obvious that August was at an end. There was hardly anyone at the beach. The summer holiday-makers had left, and the day wasn't exactly agreeable either. The weather had been rather unstable during the entire month, and the afternoon, although it wasn't raining, was sometimes shadowed by dense, white clouds. A breeze that was much too fresh for the time of day and the turbulent sea kept the few bathers stretched out on the sand and, relocating their towels, they followed the sun's rays like sunflowers in search of light.

He saw Vidal on the terrace. He'd seen him before, in the same place. He was sitting at one of the tables and seemed to be expecting someone. Every now and then he'd raise his head and look around, as if searching for something.

He went over the routes where he had to deliver goods the first week of September, and then he connected the headphones and began to play the Stratocaster. But no, the headphones isolated him from Happy, he wouldn't be able to hear her if she called. He took them off, and, at about eight o'clock, attracted by the smell of dinners that were beginning to be prepared in the restaurant, he went out onto the balcony again. It smelled of grilled seafood, and it opened up his appetite. Even so, it was still too early for dinner, and perhaps Happy, later on, would like to have something hot. She hadn't had anything to eat since lunch. But Happy ate so little, poor thing. She never managed to enjoy any type of food. Luis was permanently worried about her diet.

He lit a cigarette. He spent the whole day going in and out of the apartment for a smoke – he didn't want the tobacco to bother Happy, who, although she tolerated it, didn't smoke. He recalled with sadness, and a certain shame, a dinner he'd invited her to at the beginning of their relationship. It was at the best restaurant in town: she could have chosen any delicious dish, but preferred a simple pasta with clams. And she'd hardly eaten anything, she'd spent the dinner twirling the pasta with the tines of her fork, and, offended, he'd threatened her:

'Either you eat everything or I'll take off right now and leave you alone.'

For him it was like dealing with a little girl, and he was charmed by it. She finished her meal proudly, without a squeak. From that moment on, Luis exercised a certain tyranny over her, like a father with his daughter. They both enjoyed that game of the powerful one and the one who let herself be possessed.

He went into the small room to ask her if she'd like something for dinner. But Happy hardly opened her eyes to ask him for an analgesic. Later, when she took it, she told him to call the hotel, in case they needed something.

'Don't worry, I've already called your sister. She's coming to lunch tomorrow.'

'Federica?'

'Federica.'

'D'you know that Nuria doesn't like my sister? She said something that sounded rather harsh. What on earth does "cantankerous" mean?'

Happy was exhausted, she didn't even try to play with voices or with mixing up languages. Her fleshy lips curved downwards on her face, enlarging themselves. A bubble of saliva inflated and deflated at the right-hand corner of her lip.

'Are you sure you don't want me to take you to the doctor?'

'No, I'll be fine tomorrow. It's this stupid, unbearable weather.'

But yes, maybe it was the weather. The low clouds pressed the world against the surface of the earth. He'd also had a bit of a headache all day long.

'Or it could also be a hangover. I drank a lot yesterday,' added Happy, before doing a half-turn and sheltering herself under the pillow.

Happy didn't smoke, Happy didn't eat, but she liked to drink. And what she drank did her immediate harm. The previous night, they'd drunk too much wine with Vidal.

Vidal had invited them to dinner at his house. He was the only person in the building with whom they maintained a daily relationship, because he felt responsible for Happy. In fact, he was the one who took them to live in the building when 4E was up for sale. He wanted to have her near, and they had no problems at that time in buying it. They didn't have the big trip they'd wanted, but it was worth it, because it was a nice place, and it freed them from living up in the hotel. They didn't have to be there all day, all year, looking out for clients that might appear at any minute.

During dinner, Vidal showed them Nuria's photos.

'Do you guys recognize her?'

'No, not at all,' they answered.

Happy had fun with the story of the enigmatic neighbor, who appeared and disappeared and whom nobody knew.

'Did you bring the sketches?' asked Vidal.

'Yes,' answered Luis. 'I left them for you in the kitchen.'

Vidal got up and returned a little later with a blue folder containing dozens of sketches. They were all, all of them, sketches of seagulls done with colored waxes and charcoal pencils. At times the lines were secure, agile, furious, precise, and violent, and calm and detailed at other moments. The feathers widened as if moved by an invisible breeze, and seemed as if the person who drew them placed more interest precisely in the gentle breeze moving the feathers than in the seagull itself.

'They're good,' said Happy. 'You can almost hear them shrieking.'

'Of course they're good,' responded an admiring Vidal, as he laid them out on the table. 'They're impressive.'

'Are they Nuria's?'

'Yes, they're... do you guys know what happened to her? She disappeared one afternoon right here, on the beach. They searched and searched for her and some fishermen found her one night on one of those islands that pop up when the tide's low. Nobody knows where she was, or what she did. They found her in a boat with a half-devoured seagull. She ate one of its wings.'

'How horrible!' exclaimed Happy, and drank a little more wine – just a little more.

They stayed up until dawn, drinking, looking at Nuria's sketches and putting up with the long stories Vidal told about the photographs he'd accumulated in boxes on his shelves. It was madness, it seemed impossible that he should know everything he'd put away. But yes, if anyone touched any of his ordered-by-data boxes and asked what he kept in there, without even opening them, he'd describe their content with absolute precision. When they decided to leave, Happy was already half asleep, and Luis held her steady by hanging on to her waist.

'She ate a seagull!' said Happy, dying of laughter when she went to bed. It seemed to be something so terrible she could only take it in as humor. 'But she doesn't eat meat!'

In some way, Happy knew she was liberated. She liked Nuria, but there was something in her that hurt her, as if she knew what her debilities were and was trying to take advantage of them. She was a woman to whom nothing was easily denied. She was too full of pride. Or too harsh? When she went to bed, her head ached dreadfully, and Luis placed a bag of ice on her forehead. She fell asleep on the Indian state of Uttar Pradesh, imagining she was a lit candle floating on the Ganges River.

From the balcony Luis observed something curious. He was just going to put out his cigarette and go into the apartment to ask Happy if she'd like something for dinner, when he saw, way below on the terrace, that Nuria was sitting with Vidal. It was Nuria – there was no doubt of that – even though she was wearing her short, blonde hair more stylishly than when he'd seen her that morning. He left the balcony and, after assuring himself that Happy was asleep, he ate the remains of lunch for dinner, watched a bit of TV in the living room, and waited for night to fall.

And it was a very dark night, without a moon or stars, because the clouds covered the sky. The lights on the pier penetrated the darkness and entered the living room like worms. He put on the earphones and picked up the guitar. He played it for hours, until, without knowing why, he was shaken by a terrible loneliness: a painful silence. He wondered what was happening and it didn't take long for him to find out.

He'd stopped hearing Happy.

He got up and ran to the room. She seemed to be asleep, but her eyes were slightly open and her lips, always damp and rosy, were dry and ashy. He tried to wake her up, and it was impossible. He lay down beside her and embraced her. At dawn he took her into his arms, carried her into the living room, and laid her carefully on the sofa.

And he started to play the piano. He played a theme he'd composed for Happy a short while after he'd met her. He seemed to hear her laughing and talking to him in one of her fictitious voices. He turned his head, but she was still immobile: her hands, almost transparent, rested on her stomach and Iggy, disquieted, was sniffing at her. On the balcony, dozens of seagulls perching on the balustrade looked towards the apartment's interior in silence, as if they were the end announced by all the birds that were falling dead on the terrace.

'*Ça va, ma petite?*' he asked, and curled himself up on the chair, unable to cry.

# 32

She couldn't bear to stay there any longer. She ran down the stairs, taking the steps two by two. She rang the bell to Vidal's apartment and, since he didn't open the door, went to look for him at the restaurant. She'd arranged to have coffee with him halfway through the afternoon, but imagined that, since she was so late, he'd probably already left.

However, there he was, reading. Nuria sat down next to him. For quite a while she didn't say anything, forcing herself to repress her yearning to weep. Vidal had the grace not to look at her, not to speak to her, and not even to greet her. He continued with his reading and, from time to time, picked up a pencil and underlined a phrase, or wrote some sort of comment in the margin.

Or he drew. At times they were illuminated by the yellow light of the sun, which was beginning to move towards the ocean, and suddenly the shadow of a cloud would cover them.

There were hardly any people on the terrace. Just a few boys from the urbanization playing football under a canvas awning that moved in the breeze. When she considered herself sufficiently calmed down, she asked Vidal:

'You know me, don't you?'

Vidal shut the book with a somewhat theatrical gesture. He pushed it aside, placed the pencil on top of it, and leaned back in the chair.

'I don't know. I've seen you every month of August for the last six years. But I'm not sure if it's you or it's not you.'

He removed his glasses to rub his eyes. The pink marks they left on his nose shone with sweat. He looked at Nuria.

'During the first years you had the same haircut you have now, with the same color. It suits you.'

Nuria smiled, but soon pressed her lips together, restraining a sob. She didn't want to look into Vidal's eyes, she looked towards the estuary and distracted herself, trapped in the rays of light penetrating the large clouds. An unreal light had developed over the sea, as in a nightmare. It was almost the color of yellowed cotton, like the light on the peaches her mother kept among the bed-linen in the closet.

'Dead peaches have this color,' she said, and the gleam of a memory shone in her face.

‘Do you want to see the photos?’

On one of the chairs lay a flat box, the sort used for keeping folios in. It had her name written on it in a thick, black marker: ‘Nuria.’ She realized then that Vidal had been taking photographs of her without her knowledge, and suddenly she understood why it caused in her that feeling of rejection: she’d had the suspicion he’d been spying on her. She didn’t feel comfortable about it, but at that moment she needed to speak to him. The sun’s rays were opening greater hollows in the clouds and were like lamps illuminating specific points in a scenography, like a little fishing boat or one of those tiny islands seen only at low tide.

Vidal offered her the box. She opened it slowly, creating a certain distance between herself and whatever she might find inside it. There must have been about thirty or forty photographs in it. She spread them out over the table in the shape of a fan. She examined attentively the faces that were shown to her in color and in black and white. Although she recognized the shape of the face, the profile of the nose, the eyes, the chin... they were totally foreign to her. But, however that may be, she knew they were all inside her. Or she knew, at least, they were the faces of all the persons that inhabited her. Not even half an hour had passed since the girl with orange hair had appeared to her in the mirror, exactly like that other girl who wore her hair short and blonde, and also the one with the black mane sporting strands of violet dye.

‘What do you feel?’

‘Panic. They’re like twin sisters whom I never even knew existed until a few hours ago.’

'But you intuited them, didn't you?'

Nuria didn't answer. Vidal picked up the book and recovered from among its pages five photos which were smaller than those he'd kept in the box. He showed them to her.

'And do you know this one?'

She smiled tenderly as she held them. They were photos of herself on the beach during adolescence, with that young man. Quin! What had become of Quin? They looked so happy, the pair of them: so young, so fearless, so beautiful.

'Xoaquín Cuns!' she exclaimed suddenly, and smiled, perplexed. 'It's the young guy from the real estate agency!'

'Yes,' answered Vidal. 'He's been working there since he left high school.'

'So he knows, then!' She immediately understood the phrase 'Welcome once more,' which he'd said to her on the first day. And his inexplicable anger.

'Of course – he's seen you all these years.'

She returned to the photos, touching them with nostalgia and affection. She selected one and showed it to Vidal. It was the one where she appeared with short, blonde hair, and with a lively but sweet, ingenuous gaze, the one Bet had used to compose the mural, and also the same one she herself had kept inside the envelope.

'And why do I have a copy?'

Vidal took it from her hand and looked at it. It was, apart from the ones he'd taken of her on the beach as a teenager, the one he liked most.

'I took it of you here, at one of these tables. I developed it and gave it to you, as simple as that. Don't you remember?'

'No. I don't remember the ones on the beach, either. I can't remember almost anything.' She went silent again, and Vidal didn't bother her about it. 'I believe... I believe something happened to me here, at that time.'

Vidal doubted if he should tell her the little he knew, or if he should keep quiet. He decided not to say anything. What he could in fact tell her would only upset her even more, and wouldn't clarify anything for her.

'I don't know. It seems you fell off the cliff. That was what was deduced at the time from the wounds on your body.'

His answer didn't convince her, and obviously didn't calm her down. But what did that matter? She hadn't gone to that point to search for answers from the past. The past was within another sphere, bouncing around one of those parallel universes to which she was not permitted access.

'There's something else, Vidal... Something that happened to me in the building this month that I don't understand.'

Bowing his head slightly, Vidal leaned over towards her. He was carried away by the girl's unexpected confidence. He wanted to embrace her, kiss her, nibble those tender, round knees visible beneath her shorts. Berta, the waitress, appeared at that very moment and asked them if they wanted something to drink. They didn't respond. But yes. Almost immediately she arrived with a glass of Albariño for each of them and a plate of mussels. Nuria didn't taste the wine, and wasn't hungry, either. She'd spent the whole day floating, as if she didn't have a body. She heard her voice, but it didn't seem to come from her.

'What's going on?'

'Up on the fifth floor, there's a woman and there are children's voices and there are stains.' She fell silent, but this time the silence was tense. She was really frightened. She pressed her lips together and moved her legs under the table, shaking them. She leaned her hands on her thighs and stretched her arms to keep her back straight and perfectly vertical. She held her head up and looked off into the distance, with a shadow of terror appearing in her eyes.

'There's nobody living on the fifth floor, only you,' Vidal confirmed.

'No, that's not it. It isn't that the woman's living on the fifth floor. The woman is in my apartment, like those children that never stop talking and laughing. At first I thought she was a neighbor, but later she began to yell at me when the house was dirty. She came into my house, my room. And the children never stop making a racket, and the stains emerge all the time, regardless of how much I scrub them...' and she began to stammer and fall.

Vidal caught one of her hands and clasped it. Then she recovered that rigid posture, with the tense back and her head up. She brushed off the man's hand and continued with the detailed description of the woman in the swimsuit: her round face, the color of her hair, the wart on her neck, her small feet, her fat fingers.

'D'you remember the woman who lived in your apartment? The one who committed suicide?'

'No.'

'You must have known who she was, at least you were with me when she hit the ground. You saw her with me, dead.'

She remembered that scream she'd heard shortly after she arrived at the building, as she left the elevator. The scream and the hit on the ground. Chop. Chop, chop, and Berta's laugh when she talked about it. She pressed her head, unable to give credit to what Vidal was telling her. So what was happening was that she'd simply remembered something that had occurred years before to another Nuria, to one of those women who inhabited her? She fell silent again, thinking: It could be an explanation, but the fear was greater. All that was *inside* her. *It would always be inside her.*

'I don't know what could be happening with the stains,' Vidal continued, adopting an affected posture. 'You didn't get to know the children, and that's why I suppose you can't see them. There were two of them, and they died several years before you came here for the first time. Even so, you ought to have known at some point what had happened. I'm sure everything has a rational explanation.'

Nuria remembered the words that Induvina had said to her some time ago:

'Everything your brain does is because it just needs to. Let it go ahead and do that: allow it to. You'll feel better.'

But no, Nuria did not feel better. If everything was inside her, what other things might happen to her? She decided in a flash that she had to get out of there, one way or another.

Night was falling, and it was getting cooler. The sea breeze was almost cold, and too much of a nuisance to continue on the terrace. Vidal invited her to dinner, but she didn't accept. Although she feared going upstairs to her apartment, she had to do it. She had to go up and make some kind of a decision. When she stood up to leave, Vidal still had one final thing to tell her.

'Happy has some sketches of seagulls at home. I don't suppose you remember them either, but you drew them. Until it was sold, you always occupied her apartment in August.'

Nuria thanked him and left. She had no interest at all in recovering the sketches. She came in through the portal and called for the elevator. The huge counter looked absolutely monstrous to her, no longer ugly or out of place, as it was when she entered the building one remote evening at the end of July, but like a cadaver's dentures. And the ficus was definitively dying. And the little dolphins on the tiles were spectral figures that shivered in the dark.

The elevator arrived. She went in. As it went upwards, its weight felt more and more crushing to her. That place, where she'd been searching for light, had turned into a black, mournful well. On entering the apartment she wanted everything to be in order, and for the woman, the voices, and the stains in the corridor to have disappeared. But no, the woman was waiting for her, standing at the kitchen door. Nuria, smiling to arm herself with security and overcome fear, walked towards her in the knowledge that what actually happened was going to happen: she passed through the woman's body, which was left vibrating in the air until it suddenly disappeared, as if she'd pressed a switch. After that, she was no longer concerned about the stains or the voices, and didn't even pay attention to the sudden suspicion that, if the woman in the Lycra swimsuit was one of her holograms, then perhaps the entire apartment, and Vidal, and Happy and Luis, and the beautiful Xiabre Hotel and Federica and Iggy and she herself were only holograms.

*Everything could suddenly disappear*, but she wasn't concerned about that. Bothered by the acidic reek of the roast meat that continued on the kitchen table, and that of the magpie now completely putrefied, she made a decision: she would tidy up the apartment and leave on the first train. She cleaned everything up, but it was impossible for her to eliminate the jellyfish that floated on the walls of the small room, as alive and free as if they lived in a deep, salubrious sea. She threw away her things in a garbage bag, even the photograph, and put on the swimsuit and the indispensable clothes for the trip.

# 33

It was five in the morning when she looked at herself in the mirror above the china cabinet for the last time. She liked what she saw very much, and smiled at the girl with short, blonde hair who threw her a kiss from the palm of her hand. She picked up the garbage and abandoned the apartment. She went down in the elevator. Already at the entrance, she put her clothes behind the counter, threw the bag into the container, and went toward the beach, with her towel and her little bag in which she kept the keys and the pendant.

Her last dip before she left was waiting for her.

She swam until the break of day. In the middle of the sea, she seemed to hear the notes of Luis's piano, mixed with the ships' horns and the roar of the waves.

When she was about to get to the beach, she saw the light on in her apartment and the seagulls – all the seagulls of the estuary – perched on the railing. Surprised at the sight, she climbed up the steps of the precipice without taking her eyes away from the balcony. At the entrance, she met Federica. She had just parked her motorbike and was running as if something serious had happened. The other woman, a calmer person who'd been with her at the hotel, informed her that Happy had died the night before.

'A cerebral hemorrhage,' she explained, grasping the portal and waiting for some sort of reaction from Nuria. The spines on her tattoo were beating on her arm from the tension.

But Nuria didn't flinch. She gathered up her clothes and dressed calmly, thinking about the day they climbed up the mountain and her desire that Happy would die. 'Coincidences,' she murmured to herself. She had also secretly wished that her father would die, and it hadn't been a week before he suffered from a heart attack. 'Coincidences,' she repeated to herself. What is death, after all? To her, death would occur whenever spherical time decided to expel her from one space of life and fling her off to another space of life. It was dying and being born at the same time. Something irrelevant.

She left the building dressed in jeans, an olive-green t-shirt and a cotton sweater. She was wearing the blue canvas slippers. She wasn't taking with her anything but the pendant, the personal documents she'd sent herself by mail, and the keys to the apartment that she would hand over at the real estate agency. She would see the young Quin again and maybe apologize for not recognizing him *before*, ever. Maybe. She had almost two hours of walking to go until she reached the town; she'd have time to get herself together and decide.

She went down along the street that crossed the urbanization, solitary and silent in the first light of day. Under the rotting fruit tree, the girl in the yellow dress was eating an apple. And Nuria, or Bet, or an indefinite creature who was in that moment, was happy to see her there.

Read more fiction in English from Small Stations Press:

## **Anxos SUMAI,** THAT'S HOW WHALES ARE BORN

A young woman, who has left Galicia to go and study marine biology in Mexico (Baja California), is recalled to Galicia when it is found out that her mother is very sick. Her aunt would like her to sign some papers agreeing to take over the family business and renouncing her Mexican studies and emotional ties that she has forged in her new life. However, returning to Galicia and renewing her family ties is not exactly what the woman wants. Her mother has shut herself in her room for the last year, and relations between them have always been strained. She received more affection from a nanny, Felisa, and better advice from her uncle, Cándido. There is also an older brother, Ramón, a larger-than-life figure who has left an indelible mark in the lives of those around him, and an absent father. Will the woman's visit to see her sick mother turn out to be permanent, and will it soothe any of the festering wounds in her psyche, wounds that she has buried beneath her marine studies and a relationship with her one-time tutor? *That's How Whales Are Born* is a return to our origins, a search into the usefulness of stirring up past memories and seeking reconciliation.

**ISBN 978-954-384-073-1**

**Pedro FEIJOO,** WITHOUT MERCY

Despite their different backgrounds, Teo and Gordo have been friends since they were at school. Teo's father is head of neurosurgery at the local hospital and wants his son to follow in his footsteps. Gordo's father is a drunk, a wastrel. Gordo leaves school early and takes an apprenticeship at the local repair shop, while Teo is sent by his ambitious father to further his studies for a year in the United States. However, there is a girl in the picture. Teo is not prepared to stay behind for her, but he does abandon his studies early to return to her. The only trouble is she won't speak to him for some reason. Teo is convinced she is offended and goes to discuss the matter with Gordo. The two of them 'borrow' the garage owner's Dodge Charger, a collector's item, from the back yard and head out on a road trip, a journey without return, a desire to live in the moment, a paean to ecstasy. The only trouble is they have the police on their tail, Inspector Blanco and his men. Not to mention the local mafia, who are a little upset about an outstanding bill. The question is how long can they can keep going on a single tank of petrol? And have the two of them, such good friends, been entirely honest with each other?

ISBN 978-954-384-110-3

## **Xelís DE TORO,** FERAL RIVER

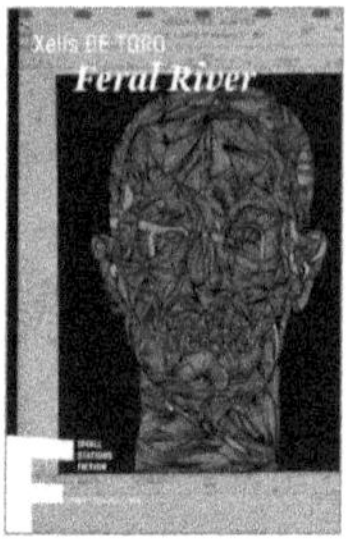


A boat with the charred body of a man crucified on its mast turns up at the mouth of the river in Romero, a town on the frontier. The boat belongs to the owner of the printing-firm that publishes the local newspaper. He engages Marqués, who is from the east coast and claims that he can write, to head upriver to find out the causes of the boatman's death. His only deckhand is a mestizo boy called Cordel who's learned his trade from the previous boatman ('What you steer isn't the boat, it's the river'). They soon reach the mission, which is staffed by a single friar, Father Bento ('He seemed to chew his words like a cow chewing grass before releasing them in short bursts'). The friar asks if Marqués has come to judge, to govern or to execute. 'To tell,' is his answer, 'I'm a writer.' Marqués, however, soon falls into a fever and has to be cured by the healing-woman from the local Aventurei Indian tribe. He realises that entering the world of the river is like clambering up a liquid wall on which there are no ledges or crannies for hands and feet to cling to. There is an obvious parallel between this narrative and Joseph Conrad's *Heart of Darkness*, in which the journey is an end in itself and the reader doesn't know what secrets the river will reveal. There is also the writer's own personal journey in search of fulfilment through his art. Marqués and Cordel will be joined on board by Rufus the Strongman and Ela, circus workers, as they struggle to come to grips with the tangle, both real and imagined, of the jungle.

**ISBN 978-954-384-105-9**

## **Anxo ANGUEIRA,** LISTING SHIP

*Listing Ship*, winner of the prestigious Xerais Prize for Novels, is a rare insight into the life of rural Galicia in the last days of the Second Spanish Republic, before the outbreak of the Spanish Civil War. We are introduced to the life of the local community centred around the village of Sernanselle (actual Manselle), southwest of Santiago de Compostela and close to the majestic Ulla river as it leaves Padrón and heads toward the Arousa estuary. There is María, who writes letters for her mother to Ramón, the son who has emigrated and whose help would be a boon around the house. Then there is Roiz Bustelo, an emigrant who has returned from Buenos Aires and is keen to invest his money in a dairy factory. Amaro, Roiz's son, who catalogues prehistoric remains that are to be found in the municipality. Camoiras, who seems to have most of his attention placed on María's pitch-black, defiant eyes. And the Master, Don Antonio, the local doctor who struggles to keep up with the latest advances in medicine. Other projects include buying a threshing machine for the entire village. But such advances will come up against the rise of fascism, the shadow of the Spanish Civil War, which threatens to spill over into violence. The novel stands as a monument to the possibilities humankind has to work together for the common good and as a lament for the self-inflicted tragedy of bigotry and antagonism. Whatever people's aspirations may be, however they may be formulated, working together, mutual understanding, has to be preferred over sticks and stones.

**ISBN 978-954-384-101-1**

For an up-to-date list of our publications, please visit
www.smallstations.com

Lightning Source UK Ltd.
Milton Keynes UK
UKHW010648221220
375698UK00001B/41

9 789543 841042